He shoved the curl back off his forehead and attempted to clear his throat. "This—whatever this was—should've never happened."

"You don't believe that any more than I do."

He was trying to come up with some sort of response, when she suddenly turned away and began gathering the dirty dishes on the coffee table.

Jarred by the sudden switch of her attention, he asked, "What are you doing?"

"Isn't it clear? I'm picking up our mess."

He stared at her in disbelief. Moments ago they'd been on their way to having sex. Now she was cleaning up their dessert dishes as though nothing had happened!

"And that's all you have to say?"

She stood and picked up the tray from the coffee table. "No. I say you're very tired. Go to bed."

* * *

MEN OF THE WEST: Whether ranchers or lawmen, these heartbreakers can ride, shoot— and drive a woman crazy

Dear Reader,

When fall arrives on Three Rivers Ranch, the foreman, Matthew Waggoner, always heads south to the Hollisters' second ranch, Red Bluff. Normally he looks forward to herding cattle to warmer, greener pastures. But for this trip, Matthew would rather eat nails. Instead of staying in the bunkhouse with the men, he's being forced to stay in the ranch house with Camille Hollister. For years he's hidden his attraction for the woman. How is he going to survive being *that* close to her?

The baby of the Hollister siblings, Camille has been living at Red Bluff ever since she suffered a broken engagement. She's well over her ex-fiancé, but she's not really looking for romance. That is, until she takes one look at Matthew. When had he turned into such a rugged hunk of a man?

It doesn't take long for the two to fall in love. But what's going to happen when Matthew has to return to Three Rivers and Camille is left behind to run her little diner in Dragoon?

Christmas is a time for miracles, and Camille realizes it's definitely going to take one to convince Matthew that the two of them belong together! I hope you'll enjoy celebrating this holiday season with the Hollisters, as Camille and Matthew learn how the best gifts in life are wrapped in love.

Merry Christmas and God bless the trails you ride!

Stella Bagwell

The Rancher's Best Gift

Stella Bagwell

◆ **HARLEQUIN**® SPECIAL EDITION

Recycling programs
for this product may
not exist in your area.

ISBN-13: 978-1-335-57426-8

The Rancher's Best Gift

Copyright © 2019 by Stella Bagwell

Printed in U.S.A.

After writing more than eighty books for Harlequin,
Stella Bagwell still finds it exciting to create new
stories and bring her characters to life. She loves
all things Western and has been married to her
own real cowboy for forty-four years. Living on the
south Texas coast, she also enjoys being outdoors
and helping her husband care for the horses, cats
and dog that call their small ranch home. The
couple has one son, who teaches high school
mathematics and is also an athletic director. Stella
loves hearing from readers. They can contact her
at stellabagwell@gmail.com.

Books by Stella Bagwell

Harlequin Special Edition

Men of the West

The Cowboy's Christmas Lullaby
Her Kind of Doctor
The Arizona Lawman
Her Man on Three Rivers Ranch
A Ranger for Christmas
His Texas Runaway
Home to Blue Stallion Ranch

The Fortunes of Texas: The Lost Fortunes

Guarding His Fortune

Montana Mavericks: The Lonelyhearts Ranch

The Little Maverick Matchmaker

Visit the Author Profile page
at Harlequin.com for more titles.

To my family and the treasured memories
of our Christmases together.

Chapter One

"Two weeks! Hell, Blake, that's a long time for me to stay down at Red Bluff."

Saddle leather creaked as Matthew Waggoner twisted around to look at Blake Hollister, his boss and manager of Three Rivers Ranch.

With a grunt of amusement, Blake leaned forward and fondly stroked the neck of the bay horse he was riding. "What's the matter? Afraid this place will fall apart without you?"

Matthew stared out at the herd of cattle grazing on tuffs of grass hidden among the thorny cacti and chaparral. The Arizona landscape was rough and rugged, especially in this area of the seventy-thousand-acre ranch. And with each day taking them nearer the end of October, the grass was getting as scarce as hens' teeth.

"Three Rivers would never miss me."

A moment passed in silence, and in the distance a coyote let out a lonesome howl, signaling that twilight was falling on the jagged peaks and deep arroyos cut by centuries of flash floods.

"No. After having you around for fourteen years, we'd never realize you were gone." He muttered a curse. "Don't give me that bull, Matthew. You know why I'm sending you to Red Bluff. I can't trust anyone with the job but you."

The Hollisters' second ranch was located in the southern part of the state, near the tiny town of Dragoon. Although at thirty-five-thousand acres, Red Bluff was only half the size of Three Rivers, it was blessed with sheltered green valleys where mama cows and calves could graze during the deepest part of winter. Each October, they shipped a large herd of cattle to Red Bluff, so this was nothing new for Matthew. Except that normally, he finished the job in two days. Not two weeks.

Lifting his hat a few inches from his head, Matthew raked fingers through the blond curls flattened to his scalp. "Are you sending the same five men with me that went last year?" he asked.

"Yes, plus one more. Scott is going along, too."

Matthew jammed the hat back down on his head and drew in a deep breath. "Guess that means we'd better take another cot for the bunk house. There's hardly enough room for five beds, but we'll jam another one in there somehow."

"Forget about an extra cot," Blake said. "I've already told Camille that you'll be staying in the big house with her."

Stunned, Matthew swung his head toward the other man. "You did what?"

"You heard me. You'll be staying in the ranch house. There's plenty of room and my sister won't bother you."

Bother him! Camille Hollister had bothered him ever since she'd grown into a woman more than ten years ago. But Blake hardly needed to know that bit of private information.

"I've always stayed in the bunkhouse with the men," Matthew reasoned. "I don't want to set myself apart from them."

Blake said, "You're the foreman and their boss. And they see you as such. Besides, you're the only man I'd trust in the house with Camille."

Careful to hide his reluctance, he said, "I don't expect your sister is going to appreciate this setup."

"Camille doesn't own or run Red Bluff Ranch. She's simply staying there until—" He broke off, a sour grimace on his face. "She gets that damned head of hers on straight," he said sourly.

Camille had left for Red Bluff more than two years ago, and since that time she'd not been back once to Three Rivers. The whole family believed she was still pining for the no-account bastard who'd broken their engagement. As for Matthew, he refrained from expressing any sort of opinion as to why the youngest member of the Hollister family had chosen to stay away. He only knew it was going to be worse than awkward sharing the ranch house with her.

"She's been down there a long time," Matthew said. "I expect by now she's thinking straight."

"Then why the hell doesn't she come home?" Blake asked, directing the question as much to himself as to

Matthew. "It's no wonder that Mom is in such a dark state of mind. And Camille could do plenty to make it better for her, but no, she's too busy thinking about herself."

Matthew inwardly winced. It wasn't often that Blake voiced such strong opinions about his siblings. Usually, he was very easygoing and especially forgiving. This ire directed at Camille was unlike him. But the weight the man carried on his shoulders as manager of Three Rivers was far more than Matthew could begin to bear.

"You think that's what your sister is doing?" Matthew asked.

"I don't know. I'm tired of trying to figure her out." He reined his horse in the direction of the ranch house. "Let's go. It's going to be dark before we get back to the ranch yard."

Matthew guided the buckskin he was riding alongside Blake's mare, and the two men urged the horses into a long trot.

Twenty minutes later, they arrived at the horse barn. As Blake had predicted, it was dark, and the ranch hands had already finished the evening chores and lit out for the bunkhouse. Except for T.J., the barn manager, and the rows of stalled horses, the cavernous building was empty.

As the two men unsaddled their mounts and put the tack away, Matthew asked, "When did you want the cows rounded up? I figure that's going to take three days, maybe more."

"Better start tomorrow," Blake told him. "The new herd should be here by then."

This was the first Matthew had heard about a new herd. "You've bought more cattle?"

Grunting, Blake shoved his saddle onto a pipe rack. "Yeah. I've been meaning to discuss the matter with you. But I've just been so damned busy, Matthew. Sorry."

"It's okay."

"No. It's not okay. You're the man who has to keep the hands going and the cattle tended to. You need to know what you're dealing with."

"So how many new cows are you talking about?"

"Five hundred more head. And I want them all to go to Red Bluff with the rest. They'll need shots and ear tags after you get them there. So figure that in with everything else you'll need to get done. Two weeks might not be enough time."

Matthew was going to make damn sure everything was wrapped up in two weeks. He wanted to get back to his own house and own bed and away from Camille Hollister as quickly as possible.

Later that same night, Camille Hollister walked across the courtyard at the back of the hacienda-style ranch house and let herself into the kitchen. After switching on a light that swung over a long table made of hand-hewn pine, she hung her jean jacket on a hook by the door, then crossed to a short row of cabinets and put a pot of coffee on to brew.

Funny, she thought, how she worked for long hours each day at a diner in Dragoon and the waitresses were constantly filling coffee cups for the customers, but Camille rarely had the chance to enjoy a cup for herself. She was too busy cooking short orders and baking pies in between. But she wasn't about to complain.

She loved her job. Even if it wasn't the sort of career her family expected of her.

While she waited for the coffee to drip into the carafe, she plucked bobby pins from the bun on top of her head and allowed her long, light brown hair shaded with a mixture of red highlights to fall down to her waist.

Massaging her scalp with one hand, she pulled a cell phone from her handbag and quickly scanned for any calls or messages she might have missed.

She found one message from Blake and punched the screen of the phone to open it.

Matthew and the crew should be there Friday. I'd appreciate it if you'd make him feel welcome.

Camille rolled her blue eyes toward the low ceiling of the kitchen. *Make Matthew feel welcome.* What the heck did her brother think she was going to do? Give the Three Rivers foreman the cold shoulder? Just because she hadn't been home in a couple of years, Blake must think she'd turned into a hateful hag or something.

Well, haven't you, Camille? For a long time after Graham asked for his engagement ring back, you didn't want to communicate with any human being. You buried yourself here on Red Bluff and rarely got off the property. And you're not exactly Miss Sociable now.

Smirking at the sardonic voice in her head, Camille walked back to the cabinet and poured herself a large mug of the coffee. As far as Matthew Waggoner went, she didn't need to be Miss Sociable. Over the past ten years, the man had probably spoken twenty words to her, and that would probably be stretching things. And the way he looked at her—she'd never been able to decide if he liked her or if she grated on his nerves.

Either way, she'd not given the man much thought these past couple of years. But then her family would say she'd not given anyone much thought, except for herself.

And maybe they were right, she pondered as she sat down at the table and propped her feet on the chair next to her. She had gone a little crazy when Graham had jilted her. But she'd gotten over him ages ago. She was getting on with her life now and she was doing it without a man. And without her family breathing down her neck. It felt good. And that's the way she intended for things to stay.

Picking up the phone, she typed in a reply to her brother: Don't worry. I'll roll out the red carpet for Matthew.

Friday evening when Camille arrived home from work, the ranch yard was buzzing with activity. Pickup trucks, along with several semi-truck cattle haulers, were parked at different angles near the barn area. Portable pens had been erected next to the permanent wooden corrals to hold the extra cattle that were being unloaded.

Working dogs were barking and nipping at the heels of the lagging cattle, while misplaced calves bawled for their mamas to find them. Dust boiled high in the air, men shouted to communicate above the din of noise, and horses neighed to each other.

For a couple of minutes, Camille stood watching the activity, and then an odd thing happened. A hard lump lodged in her throat and tears filled her eyes to the point where the ranch yard became nothing but a watery blur.

Cursing to herself, she entered the house and wiped her eyes. Darn it, she'd been done with tears a long time ago. And she sure as heck wasn't homesick. No, she'd spent twenty-six years of her life on Three Rivers and that was enough. She loved it here on Red Bluff. But seeing the men on horseback, the cattle and dogs had all reminded her of her late father, Joel. Next to his wife and children, ranching had been his deepest joy and if he'd still been alive, he'd be out there right now with the rest of the men, doing the job he'd loved.

Nearly nine years had passed since her father had died, yet Camille still endured unbearable moments when she longed to see his grinning face and feel his comforting arms around her. She'd been a daddy's girl and once he'd died nothing had been the same.

Giving herself a hard mental shake, Camille walked straight to her bedroom and stripped off her slacks and blouse that were permeated with the odors of fried food and burnt cooking oil. It being Friday, the diner had been extra busy all day. She'd lost count of the burgers and chicken strips she'd cooked today. Now, instead of relaxing with a cup of coffee and the book she'd been reading, she had to shower and get ready for Matthew Waggoner.

Oh well, it would only be for a couple of weeks, she reminded herself. Surely she could put up with the man's company for that long.

The Red Bluff ranch house was built in a square with a low sandstone wall and a slatted iron gate serving as an entryway at the back of the structure. On the bottom floor, a covered porch ran the whole length of the house, while the second floor was structured with a roofed balcony. The thick walls were covered with stucco and painted a dark beige, while the flat-style roof consisted of board shingles weathered to a pale gray. The windows and doors were framed with wood that had once been black, but had long ago faded to a charcoal color.

It was a gorgeous example of a traditional hacienda ranch house and made even more charming by the inner courtyard landscaped with succulents, a tall saguaro and three large Joshua trees. Years ago, the Hollisters would often drive down in the dead of winter and enjoy a few days of the warmer climate. But plenty had changed since then. Joel was gone and all of the Hollister siblings, except for Camille, were married with children. And she would've been a wife by now, too, if Graham Danby hadn't changed his mind about marrying her.

That last thought was going through Matthew Waggoner's mind as he let himself through the wrought-iron gate that connected the sandstone wall and walked around the edge of the courtyard to the back door of the house.

Although he had keys to both front and back doors, Matthew was loath to use either one. Even though the house didn't belong solely to Camille, it was currently her residence, and he didn't want to barge in as though he had a right to the place.

After knocking on the back door, he glanced over his shoulder to a view of the ranch yard. From where Matthew stood, he could see a corner of the bunkhouse. Smoke was coming from the chimney and though it was well after ten, lights blazed in the windows. Barely fifteen minutes had passed since Matthew and the other men had called it a night. Now he figured they were all pestering Curly, who'd reluctantly taken on the job of cook, to fix them something to eat. As for Matthew, he didn't care if he ate a bite of anything. After the exhausting day he'd put in, all he wanted was a mattress and pillow.

The sound of the door creaking open caused his head to turn back to the house, and he suddenly found himself staring straight into Camille Hollister's face.

"Hello, Matthew."

"Hello, Camille."

A long stretch of silence passed, and all the while Matthew could hear a pack of coyotes yipping in the far distance, while closer to the house the penned cattle continued to bawl in protest.

Red Bluff was wild, rugged land and far from town or any kind of civilization, yet Camille lived here alone. What kind of twenty-eight-year-old woman made such a choice? The kind that was still nursing a broken heart?

He was trying to answer that question as she pushed the door wide and gestured for him to enter.

"Please, come in," she said. "I hope you haven't been knocking long. I dozed off on the couch. And the walls of the house are so thick it's hard to hear outside noises."

"I've only been here a minute." He stepped into the kitchen and blinked as she switched on a light hanging over the table. The room basically looked the same as it had the last time he'd been in the house, and that had been at least five or six years ago when Blake and Maureen had come down to stay a few days during fall roundup. For the past couple of years since Camille had moved in, Matthew and the men had steered wide of the ranch house.

"Sorry it's so late," he apologized. "I hope you didn't wait up just to let me in. I have a key."

She shut and locked the door, then walked over to where he stood. Matthew desperately tried not to notice the soft scent of flowers emanating from her hair and skin. It swirled around him and pulled his gaze to the gentle features of her face. She'd always been beautiful, but tonight she seemed to be even lovelier. Or was that because he'd not seen her in two long years?

"I didn't know whether you had a key or not. But it's no big deal," she said. "I usually don't get into bed until eleven anyway. Uh, would you like something to eat, or drink?"

"Don't worry about feeding me," he said. "I can fend for myself."

Her lips pursed together as though his answer offended her. "I didn't ask whether you could fend for yourself. It's a simple question. Are you hungry?"

She sounded so much like her mother, Maureen, he very nearly smiled. "Put like that, then yes, I'm hungry. But it's late and I'm tired. I'll grab something in the morning."

To his complete surprise, she clamped a hand around his arm. "Come with me," she said in a tone that warned him not to argue.

With her hand still burning a ring around his forearm, she guided him out of the kitchen. Before they reached the living room, she turned to the left and down a long hallway. Soft nightlights glowed from the baseboards and illuminated the rich tile on the floor. The walls were decorated with huge framed prints of the

Hollisters and the ranch hands doing various jobs here on Red Bluff.

She came to a sudden stop and pointed to one of the photos. "Just in case you're wondering if you're in any of these, here's one of you and Daddy. Remember that day?"

Shoving the brim of his hat back off his forehead, he stepped forward and peered at the picture. The image struck him hard.

"I've never seen this before," he said, his voice thick. "That horse is Dough Boy. He always bucked when you first got on him, so you had to be ready. Your father was riding him that day. We'd been gathering cattle in Lizard Canyon. Dough Boy was a real gentleman that day and Joel joked that he was the only cowboy on the ranch who could ride him."

"Yeah," she murmured thoughtfully. "Isn't it ironic that Daddy was on Major Bob the day he was killed instead of Dough Boy?"

Ironic? No. Matthew's views on Joel Hollister's death were no different than those of the family. No matter the horse he'd been riding, Joel would've died that day because someone had meant to kill him.

"I'd rather remember other days. Not that one," Matthew told her.

He heard her long sigh, and then the hand on his arm was urging him toward the nearest door to their right.

"This will be your room while you're here. I could've given you one overlooking the courtyard, but I figured you'd rather have the best mattress than the best view."

She pushed the door open and gestured for him to enter. Matthew felt like he was stepping into the room of a Mexican villa. The dark wooden furniture was heavy, the bed fashioned with four posts that nearly touched the ceiling. The tall headboard was intricately carved with the images of blazing suns, fighting bulls and trailing moonflowers. At the windows, thick burgundy-colored drapes were pulled to show a moonlit view of the desert mountains.

"Is that one bag all you have?" she asked.

"No. I have another case in the truck, but I don't need to unpack it tonight."

She nodded. "Well, just put your things wherever you like. There's a private bath through the door over by the closet. Make yourself at home."

He moved into the room while thinking with each step that he didn't belong in this house with this woman. They were both too rich for his blood. But being here was Blake's order and Matthew would bend over backwards to make the man happy. Not because he was his boss, but because Blake and his three brothers were like his blood brothers and always would be.

"Thanks. This is nice." He placed his duffel bag on the green-and-burgundy-patterned spread, then glanced over to her. "I—uh—think I ought to tell you that it wasn't my idea for me to stay here in the house."

"I never imagined it was."

Although he didn't know why, he felt the need to further explain. "Blake sent an extra man this time. There wasn't enough room for another bed in the bunkhouse."

She shrugged. "No problem. You won't bother me. And I'm gone most of the time so I shouldn't bother you."

Maybe not, but she sure as hell was bothering him right now. Strange how he'd not remembered her looking exactly like this. Her hair had grown and now reached the back of her waist. She was wearing some sort of loose flowing pants made of flower-printed material. The top that matched had a low V-neck, and when she turned a certain way he could see a hint of cleavage. Before she'd left Three Rivers she'd been extremely slender. Now she was voluptuous and it sure looked good on her, he thought.

"Don't worry. The men and I have so much work to do while we're down here that I doubt our paths will cross much."

Her plush lips curved into something close to a smile. "Go wash up and come back to the kitchen. I'll have something for you to eat."

He wanted to argue with her, but he knew it would be a losing battle. And why bother? After tonight, he expected she'd leave him to see after himself.

"All right. Thanks."

Chapter Two

Back in the kitchen, Camille opened the fridge and pulled out a ribeye steak she'd been marinating. As she heated an iron skillet and tossed in several hunks of butter, her mind spun with thoughts of Matthew Waggoner.

When had he turned into such a hunk of a man? She'd not exactly remembered him being so broad through the shoulders, his waist so trim, or his legs being that long and corded with muscles. And that blond, blond hair. He used to wear it buzzed up the sides. Now it was long and curled against the back of his neck and around his ears. But it wasn't just the hair or the breadth and strength of his body that had caught Camille's attention. There was something different about his rugged features. Perhaps it was the hardened glint in his gray eyes or the unyielding thrust of his jaw. Whatever it was, he looked too damned sexy for her peace of mind.

A mocking laugh trilled inside her head. *Just what I thought, Camille. You weren't really serious when you swore off men for the next ten years. You take one look at the Three Rivers foreman and you start swooning like a silly schoolgirl. Snap out of it, girl! You have nowhere else to run to!*

Run? No, Camille thought as she shoved the voice right out of her head. She wasn't going anywhere. And she wasn't afraid of her heart or anything else getting tangled up with Matthew. She'd known the man since she was a teenager and they'd hardly been anything more than acquaintants. Nothing was different now. Nothing at all.

She was still frying the steak when Matthew returned to the kitchen. He'd not changed out of the clothes he'd been working in, but he'd knocked off most of the dust. The long sleeves were rolled up to expose thick forearms burnt to the same nut-brown color of his face. He'd left his hat behind and Camille decided he must have run wet hands through his hair. Damp tendrils fell across his forehead and tickled the tops of his ears.

Just looking at him caused a flutter in her stomach.

"Go ahead and have a seat at the table, Matthew. Would you like a glass of wine or a beer?"

He pulled out a chair at the end of the table and sank into it. "A beer would be nice."

She carried a tall bottle and a glass mug over to the table and set both in front of him. "If you're wondering if I've turned into a drinker, don't worry. I mostly keep beer and wine to cook with."

"I wasn't thinking anything like that," he said.

She went back over to the gas range and switched off the blaze under the steak. By now the French fries were done and she loaded a pile of them along with the steak onto a large plate, then gathered a small bowl of tossed salad from the fridge.

When she set the whole thing in front of him, he cut his gray eyes up to her. "This is overdoing it, Camille."

Her heart was beating fast and it had nothing to do with his words and everything to do with the way he was looking at her, the way he smelled, the way his masculine presence filled up the small kitchen.

"What's wrong? I cooked the steak too long?"

He shook his head. "This is not a part of the deal."

"What deal? I didn't know we had a deal?"

He made a flustered sound as he reached for the knife and fork she'd placed next to his plate. "I'm not your guest. I'm here to work cattle."

"You don't have to tell me why you're here, Matthew." She left the table and walked over to the cabinets. "You've been doing this for years."

Yes, fourteen years to be exact. When Matthew had first gone to work for Three Rivers Ranch, Joel had brought him and four other hands down here to Red Bluff. The work had been exhausting, but the special time working closely with Joel had changed Matthew's life. He'd found the father he'd always needed and the home he'd never had.

She plunked a bottle of salad dressing along with a pair of salt and pepper shakers in front of him. "You want any ketchup or steak sauce?"

Her question pulled him out of his memories and with a tired sigh, he pulled the plate toward him. "No, thanks. This is good."

Once he started to eat, he thought she might leave

the kitchen and go on about her business. Instead, she pulled out the chair angled to his right elbow.

"Looks like Blake sent plenty of cattle this time. I saw the extra pens."

He glanced at her. "He's been on a buying spree. When prices drop, your brother takes advantage."

She smiled wanly. "Blake always did know how to turn a profit."

The steak melted in his mouth, a fact that surprised Matthew. He would've never guessed Camille could do much in the kitchen. Reeva had ruled as the Three Rivers house cook for long before Camille had been born and the woman wasn't the sort who wanted to share the domain.

"I guess you've taken to living here on Red Bluff," he said. "You've been gone from Three Rivers for a long time."

She slanted him a shrewd look. "Did my family send you on a fishing expedition?"

He chewed another bite of steak before he answered. "That's funny. But I'm too tired to laugh."

"What's funny about it? You're a part of the family. You know as well as I do that they're trying to figure me out—or come up with a way to get me back to Three Rivers."

He glanced over to see a smirk on her face, but whether her ire was directed at him or her family he couldn't guess.

"I didn't ask you anything," he said. "I only made an observation. Guess the subject of you living here on Red Bluff is a prickly one."

"You know it is."

Deciding it took too much energy to talk to this woman, he focused on finishing the food on his plate.

Quietness settled around them until she spoke again. "Sorry, Matthew. I didn't mean to sound so—defensive. It's just that I'm beyond weary of answering my family's questions. They can't accept that I want to live here and leave it at that."

"They think you're still pining over that Danby guy and that makes them worry about you."

Her lips pressed to a thin line. "For your information and theirs, Graham Danby is a thing of the past," she said firmly. "I'm perfectly happy living single and I have no interest in the male population in Yavapai County, or here in Cochise County, or anywhere else for that matter."

"Okay."

His simple response didn't ease the frown on her face.

She said, "Since my personal life seems to be fair game, maybe it's time I asked you a few questions. Like have you ever gotten over your failed marriage with Renee?"

Although he was stunned that she'd brought up the subject of his divorce, he realized he couldn't tell her to mind her own business. Not without looking like an ass.

"Renee who?"

She snorted. "You can't fool me, Matthew. That was what—at least ten years ago and you've never remarried. You're either still crazy in love with the woman or too scared to try marriage again."

He stabbed his fork into the fries. "Your first assumption is dead wrong. Your second one is not exactly right, either."

Her vivid blue eyes continued to peruse his face, and Matthew wondered what she was looking for. A sign of weakness? A crack in his armor? Well, if anyone could find it, she could.

He said, "I'll admit that when Renee and I divorced it knocked me off my feet."

"It shouldn't have," she said bluntly. "I could've told you before you ever married her that she was all fluff."

He scowled at her. "How would you know that? You were only a teenager back then."

"A girl doesn't have to reach the age of twenty before she learns how to spot a female piranha."

He grunted. "Men are slow learners."

A faint smile touched her face. "The last I heard you were dating a redhead from Yarnell. Are you getting serious about her?"

"No. I haven't seen her in more than a year. And I'm not planning on getting serious about anyone. I'm going to leave marriage up to you and Vivian, and your brothers."

Her face went void. "Leave me off that list, Matthew. The chance of me ever marrying is as about as good as snow falling here on Red Bluff. And that'll be a cold day in hell."

The bitterness in Camille's voice matched the feelings he'd carried around inside him for all these years. He understood the humiliation she'd gone through when Danby had chosen another woman over her. He'd felt that same sting when Renee had left him high and dry.

"So what do you with yourself now?" he asked. "I imagine it's awfully quiet around here when the ranch hands aren't around."

Faint surprise arched one of her delicate brows. "You

mean none of the family has mentioned my job to you? That's a shocker."

He shook his head. "No. You found an office job over in Benson or Tucson?"

Rolling her eyes, she got up from the table and walked over to the cabinets located directly behind him.

"Lord no! I'd have to be starving to death before I ever work in an office again."

He glanced over his shoulder to see she was filling a coffeemaker with grounds and water.

"Why? That is the reason you went to college," he stated the obvious. "What are you going to do? Let all that education go to waste?"

He didn't know why he'd let himself be sucked into such a personal conversation with this woman. Maybe because in the quieter moments of his life, he'd often thought of her and hoped she was happy.

With the coffee dripping, she walked back over to the table and took her seat. "No. That isn't why I went to college. I worked to get my degree in business management because that's what Daddy wanted for me and I promised him I would."

"He died shortly after you graduated high school. He would've never known if you'd chosen to take a different path."

"Maybe not. But I would have known it. I made a promise to him and I wasn't about to break it."

Her loyalty to her father didn't surprise Matthew. Even though Camille had never been the cowgirl that her mother and sister were, she'd been very close to Joel, and he to her. Perhaps because she was the baby of the family, or perhaps it was the fact that she was so different from Vivian that Joel had been extra protective of his youngest.

"So if you don't have an office job, what are you doing?" he asked.

"I'm a cook in a diner over by Dragoon."

Hearing she'd been hired on as a cook was almost too much for his tired brain to register. "The population can't be three hundred there. I wasn't aware it had an eating place. I only remember it having a few houses and old buildings."

"It's there. Not far from the interstate. Lots of folks from Wilcox traveling through to Benson and Tucson stop to eat. The building isn't much to look at and we mostly just have short orders, but the customers seem to enjoy it and I love working there."

The moment she'd started to talk about her job, the taut expression on her face had relaxed.

"To tell you the truth, Camille, I didn't even know you could cook until tonight." He gestured to his empty plate. "By the way, it was delicious."

"Thanks. That's what I like to hear." She leaned back in the chair and crossed her arms across her breasts. "I think Mom regrets that Reeva allowed me to help her in the kitchen. I probably don't have to tell you that she expects more out of me than being a cook."

"Why? Because you're a Hollister?"

She wrinkled her nose. "Isn't that enough?"

"Yeah," he said after a moment of thought. "It's a lot to live up to."

She smiled and the expression on her face was suddenly sunny and sweet and exactly the way he remembered her when he'd first come to Three Rivers. The sight sent a poignant pang rifling through him and he hated himself for being so sentimental. Especially with Camille. Of all the Hollister siblings, she'd often been more of a rebel than Holt.

She said, "I actually think you understand."

"Why wouldn't I? I'm not a Hollister, but Joel always expected a lot from me. More than I thought I was capable of. It was never easy trying to live up to the expectations he had of me. I tried. But I honestly don't know if it was ever enough."

"It was more than enough. You were like a son to him."

Hearing those words from Camille twisted something deep inside him, and he wondered why seeing her again was bringing up thoughts he'd tried so hard to keep in the past.

She picked up his empty plate and carried it over to the sink. While she was gone, Matthew rubbed both hands over his face. These next two weeks were going to be even longer than he'd first imagined, he thought. And he was wondering just how early he'd need to get up in the morning to avoid running into her before he left the house. Or how late he would need to stay out at night until she went to bed.

Her fragrance drifted to him and he dropped his hands to see she'd returned to the table with a small plate of chocolate pie and a cup of coffee.

"I realize you're tired, but I thought you might like dessert."

"Did you make this?" he asked.

She gave him a half smile. "Yes. I bake pies for the diner, too. They're a big hit with the customers, so the owner pays me extra for doing it."

She's simply staying on Red Bluff until she gets her head on straight.

Blake couldn't be more wrong, Matthew thought as the man's remark came back to him. Camille didn't look or sound like she was suffering a broken heart. In fact, she appeared to be content. If the Hollisters were expecting her to return to Three Rivers to cry on their shoulders, they were all in for a rude surprise.

"This is very good," he said after he'd taken the first bite. "It tastes like Reeva's."

"Thanks. That's the best compliment you could've given me."

"Are you not having any?"

"No. I've already eaten my quota of sweets for today."

She propped her elbows on the table and rested folded hands beneath her chin. "So, what's been happening at Three Rivers lately? Mom mostly keeps me informed, but I think she purposely avoids talking about certain things."

"Like what?"

"Like my brothers' and sister's babies. She thinks hearing about them makes me sad because I don't have any." She moved her head back and forth. "And I guess in a way, it does. But if I'm meant to have children I'll have them in due time."

She had the frankness of her mother and the practicality of her father, Matthew thought. Together, she was unlike any of her siblings.

"All the children are fine and it won't be long until Holt's baby arrives. It's going to be strange to hear him called Daddy."

"I'm very happy for him. And Isabelle is wonderful.

She's the perfect match for him," she said, then gave him a long, pointed look. "So, what about my brothers and their search into Dad's death?"

Matthew shook his head. "You know about that?"

"Mom and my brothers don't talk to me about it, but Vivian does. She says Mom clams up if she asks her anything about it and our brothers are obsessed with the subject."

"What do you think?" he asked curiously. "That they should continue to search for answers or leave the whole thing be?"

Sighing, she closed her eyes, and Matthew used the moment to study her face. She'd always had beautiful features but now they held a maturity that made her even more attractive. All he could think was how stupid Graham Danby had been to ask for his engagement ring back and how lucky Camille was that he had.

"Answers would be good, I suppose," she finally said. "But in the end it won't bring Daddy back. That's harder for me to live with than the not knowing."

"Your brothers want justice."

"Don't you mean vengeance?"

"Maybe. I'd definitely like to serve up a little vengeance of my own."

He rose from the chair and picked up the dirty dessert plate along with his cup. "Thanks for the meal, Camille. I really need to get to bed. The men are going to be saddled up by five thirty. That's going to come pretty early."

Nodding, she rose along with him and reached for the dishes in his hands. "I'll take care of those. You go on."

He started out of the room, then paused at the doorway to look back at her. "Camille, from now on you really need to let me fend for myself."

The faint smile on her face said it didn't matter what he said. Ultimately she'd do whatever she wanted to do.

"Good night, Matthew."

"Good night, Camille."

The next morning at the diner in Dragoon, Camille slid a stack of pancakes and a pair of over-easy eggs onto a warm plate, placed it on a tall counter and slapped a bell to alert Peggy that the order was ready.

The waitress immediately snatched up the plate and hurried away. Camille reached for the next order and recognized with a sigh of relief there wasn't a next order. For the moment she was caught up.

"Wow! What a run. I haven't had time to draw in a good breath!" Peggy exclaimed as she pushed through the swinging door and into the small kitchen. "Where are all of these people coming from?"

Camille sank onto a wooden stool and looked over at the tall woman with a messy black bun pinned to the top of her head. In her early thirties, with big brown eyes and a wide smile that hid all kinds of disappointments in her life, Peggy had become a dear friend to Camille.

"The few times I glanced out to the dining area, I didn't spot one familiar face. They must all be travelers."

"Hmm, good thing, I guess. If we had to depend on customers from Dragoon, we might as well close up the doors." She looked over at Camille and shook her head. "Honey, I'll never understand why you're wasting yourself in this lonely little spot in the desert."

She smiled wanly at her friend. "Because I like this

little lonely spot in the desert. I've tried the big city thing. The traffic and hustle and bustle. The business suits and high heels. Yes, I made a nice salary, but it wasn't worth it to me."

Peggy tightened the bobby pins holding her bun. "Hmm. I wouldn't mind trying it someday. Just to see what it was like to live in a house that wasn't filled with dust and to smell like a woman instead of burnt coffee and cooking grease."

"Who cares about dust?" Camille retorted. "And if men were honest, most of them would say they'd rather have a woman who smelled like food instead of flowers."

"And who around here wants a man?" Peggy asked with a cynical laugh. "I certainly don't! And even if I did, the single male population around here is darned scarce."

Camille thoughtfully regarded her friend. If Peggy took more pains with her appearance, she'd be a knockout. But makeup or a hairdo wouldn't take the jaded shadows from her eyes. Only deep-down happiness could do that.

"So it is, but that doesn't mean you should stop looking. You've told me before how much you'd like a child of your own," Camille reasoned. "You can't very well make one without a man."

Peggy slanted her a tired look. "There's always a fertility clinic."

Camille couldn't believe her friend would actually go to that length to have a baby on her own. "Are you saying you're ready to do that?"

Peggy shrugged. "Wouldn't that be better than putting up with a creep who spouts words of love, then cheats every chance he gets?"

From what Peggy had told her, she'd been engaged once, but the guy had turned out to be a verbal abuser and she'd dumped him before the wedding plans could get started. After that misjudgment, she'd married a car salesman from Tucson, but a week after they'd gotten back from their honeymoon, he'd cheated on her. Given the briefness of the marriage, she'd gotten an annulment. Now she looked at men as though they all had horns and a forked tongue.

"Peggy, there's a good man out there just waiting for you to find him."

Peggy's short laugh was mocking. "Coming from you, Camille, that's very funny. A beauty like you, hiding yourself away." She pushed away from the work counter and started out of the kitchen, only to pause at the swinging doors. "By the way, what are you doing tonight? I thought I'd drive over to Benson and try to find something to wear to Gideon's Halloween party. Wanta come?"

"Gideon is having a party?"

Gideon was a seventy-five year old war veteran and widower who bussed the tables here at the diner. He was a happy-go-lucky guy, but Camille couldn't picture him throwing a Halloween party.

"His grandchildren are coming to visit and he wants to do something special for them, so I've offered to lend him a hand."

Any other time, Camille would have given her friend a quick yes. But she hated to think of Matthew dragging himself in tonight, exhausted and hungry, and her not being there to take care of him.

What the heck are you thinking, Camille? Matthew isn't your man. He's a grown man who's lived alone for years. He doesn't need you or anyone to take care of him!

The sardonic voice going off in her head couldn't have been more right, Camille thought. She'd be more than stupid to start planning her life around Matthew. In two weeks he'd be gone back to Three Rivers and she wouldn't see him again until next year. On the other hand, if she did want to spend any time with the foreman, she needed to make the most of the next fourteen days while he and the roundup crew were at Red Bluff.

Rising from the stool, she picked up a spatula. As she scraped grease and meat particles from the flat grill, she said, "Thanks for asking, Peggy, but the crew from Three Rivers is at Red Bluff now and I feel like I need to be there."

Peggy frowned. "Be there for what? I've never known of you doing ranch work."

Normally, the woman's remark would have rolled off Camille's back, but for some reason it stung today. "Well, I have been known to ride a horse and herd cows. I just haven't done that sort of thing in a long time. Anyway, I just meant they might need me to run errands or something."

The waitress shrugged. "Okay, you go ahead and play cowgirl. I've got to find something spooky to wear."

Peggy disappeared through the swinging doors, and Camille dropped the spatula and swiped a hand across her forehead. She honestly didn't know what was coming over her.

Ever since Matthew had shown up at her door last

night, she'd been thrown into a strange state of mind. All of a sudden she'd forgotten about keeping a cool distance from the man. Seeing him had evoked all sorts of poignant memories. Seeing him had been like a sweet homecoming, and his company had filled her with a sense of belonging. Which didn't make any sense. She'd never been close to the Three Rivers foreman before. So why did she want to be close to him now?

The cowbell over the door to the diner clanged, breaking into Camille's thoughts, and moments later, Peggy was pinning up two orders for chicken-fried steak.

Glad for the distraction, Camille went to work. But it wasn't enough to make her forget about seeing Matthew again.

Chapter Three

The five ranch hands working with Matthew on Red Bluff were a good, dependable crew ranging in ages from twenty to sixty. Curly, the designated cook for the bunch, was the oldest, and Pate, a tall lanky cowboy with a shock of black hair and a lazy grin, was the youngest. In between, there was Scott, in his midthirties and a wizard with a lariat. Abel, a redhead with a face full of freckles and a boisterous personality to match, was 25, but already experienced in ranch work. TooTall was a Native American from the Yavapai tribe and a skilled horseman, who often worked alongside Holt. A quiet loner, TooTall had never told anyone his age. Just by looking, Matthew guessed him to be thirty, but he wouldn't be surprised to learn he was much older.

This morning Matthew had ordered Curly and Abel to remain behind at the ranch yard to tend to the penned cattle, while the others rode with him to hunt for steers. The sky was cloudless, and by midday the Arizona sun was blazing down on the jagged hills and piers of red rock that made up the southern range of the ranch.

For the past few hours, Matthew and the men had been rounding up steers from the thick patches of chaparral and prickly pear. So far they'd gathered twenty head and penned them in a wooden corral built next to a tall rock bluff. It had been a productive morning, but Matthew knew for certain there were at least ten more steers somewhere on this section of range. It wouldn't necessarily hurt to turn the cows and calves in with those last ten, but Blake wanted them back at Three Rivers and Matthew wasn't the kind of man to leave anything undone.

"My arms feel like a pair of pincushions," Pate said. "I'll bet I've been stuck fifty times with thorns and pear spines."

Matthew looked over at the young cowhand sitting next to him beneath the meager shade of a Joshua tree. A half hour ago, the group had stopped for lunch, and now the horses stood dozing and resting in the shade while the men finished the food they'd pulled from their saddlebags.

"Make sure you get all those thorns out tonight," Matthew told him. "They'll fester if you don't."

"I should've worn my jacket, but it's too damned hot." Pate turned his head and squinted at the western horizon. "If you ask me, it's going to take another day or two to find the other steers. There's too many arroyos and rock bluffs where they can hide. And we've not spotted hide nor hair of them."

Pate was a good worker, but he still had lots to learn.

The same way Matthew had all those years ago when Joel had taken him under his wing. "Whether it takes a week or ten days, we'll get them," he told the young cowboy.

Pate whistled under his breath. "At that rate it'll be Thanksgiving before we get back to Three Rivers!"

Matthew's grunt was full of humor. "What's the matter? You don't like sleeping on a cot, or eating Curly's pork 'n' beans?"

"I'm not particularly fond of either one." The young man grimaced, then slanted Matthew a sly glance. "Guess you were comfy in the big hacienda. What's that place like inside?"

"Nice."

Pate frowned. "That's all you can say? Nice?"

Matthew shrugged. "I didn't take that much notice to the house."

"No. Don't guess you would when you got Camille Hollister to look at."

Matthew stabbed him with a steely glare. "I'm going to forget that you said that, Pate. But if I ever hear it again, I'll knock your damned head off."

The young cowboy looked stunned and just a little scared. "What the hell is wrong with you?"

"You heard me."

Matthew stuffed the leftovers of his lunch into a set of saddlebags, then carried them over to the dun he was riding. After tying them onto the back of the saddle, he made a circling motion with his arm.

"Let's go. We'll search this draw until we reach the southern fence. If we don't find anything there, we'll haul the ones we have into the ranch yard and start again tomorrow."

Nearly an hour later, Matthew was riding along the edge of a rocky wash when Pate reined his horse alongside him.

"You find anything?" Matthew asked him.

"No. None of us have seen a sign of a steer." He lifted his hat and swiped a hand through his thick black hair. "I—uh—I just wanted to tell you I'm sorry if I offended you earlier. I wasn't meaning to be disrespectful about Miss Hollister. I just meant—well, I've never met her, but some of the men say she's really pretty."

Matthew let out a long sigh. Pate couldn't possibly know that he'd spent all night and most of today trying to get Camille out of his head, but everywhere he looked he was seeing her face and thinking about all the things she'd said to him. She wasn't the same woman who'd left Three Rivers more than two years ago and this new Camille was eating at his common sense.

"Forget it, Pate. My fuse is running short and—staying in the ranch house is a prickly subject with me."

"Why? I mean, this is hard work. You deserve the extra comfort."

"I don't like being away from you men."

"But you're the boss."

"Yeah. And sometimes that means doing things you don't want to do."

Pate shook his head. "No need to worry about us men, Matthew. We won't let you down. When we get back to Three Rivers, Blake will be proud of the job we've done down here."

Proud. Pate's word drifted through Matthew's mind later that night as he let himself in the back door of the ranch house. Would Blake be proud if he knew his foreman had carnal thoughts toward his sister? Like hell. He'd probably be hopping mad. Or would he?

The Hollisters were far from snobs. Even though they owned two of the biggest ranches in the state of Arizona, they treated everyone as equals. Unless a person crossed them, which didn't happen often.

"Matthew, is that you?"

He was about to turn down the hallway to his room when he heard Camille's voice and looked over his shoulder to see her standing in the arched doorway that led to the living room. Tonight she was wearing a long flowing skirt with swirls of green and purple and turquoise. Her blouse was green velvet and cinched in at the waist with a belt of silver conchas. If possible she looked even lovelier than she had last night, and the sight of her caused his stomach to clench in a nervous knot.

"Yes. I used my key so I wouldn't disturb you."

She walked down the hallway to where he stood, and for one wild second he wondered how she would react if he pulled her into his arms and kissed her. It was something he'd often thought about over the years. Kissing Camille. Making love to Camille. It was a crazy fantasy and one that he definitely couldn't act upon.

"Trying to sneak past me?" she asked.

Her smile was shrewd, but held just enough warmth to let him know it didn't matter if he had been trying to avoid her. One way or the other, she was going to catch him.

He shrugged. "It didn't work, did it?"

She shook her head. "When you get washed up I have something for you in the kitchen."

"Camille, I told you—"

"I know what you told me," she interrupted. "But

as long as you're here, you're going to eat what I give you. No arguments."

His nostrils flared at the sweet fragrance drifting from her body. "It's Saturday night. Why aren't you out doing whatever it is you do for entertainment?"

She smiled. "I've already had plenty of entertainment at the diner today. Why? Are you planning on going out tonight? They've opened a nice club on the edge of Benson. I hear they have a great live band. You might want to check it out and kick up your heels."

It was already past ten. Did she think he was up to that sort of nightlife after sitting in the saddle all day, popping brush?

"I'm thirty-three, not twenty-three, Camille."

Laughing, she turned and left him standing there staring after her.

When Matthew appeared in the kitchen some fifteen minutes later, Camille set a plate of enchiladas, Spanish rice and refried beans in front of him, along with several warm flour tortillas.

"I suppose you just happened to whip this up in your spare time," he said as he took his seat at the table.

"Listen Matthew, don't go getting the idea that my cooking is something special I'm doing just for you. I'm not a sandwich person. Nor do I like things out of a box. I cook for myself. You get what's left over. Does that make you feel any better?"

"Okay. I won't say another word about it."

She clapped her hands together. "Yay! We're finally getting somewhere."

She placed a beer in front of him, then opened one for herself and took the same seat she'd sat in last night.

Apparently she had no plans to leave him alone while he ate.

"You could eat in the dining room if you like," she offered. "But it's much nicer in here."

"This is fine with me."

"So, how did things go today?" she asked. "I noticed there were lots of cattle still penned out by the barns."

Her long hair was loose and it slid over her shoulder as she rested a forearm against the table. When he'd first gone to work at Three Rivers, Camille had been in high school. She'd worn her hair bobbed to chin-length and it had matched her perky personality. The years since had transformed her into a very sensual female. One who was impossible for Matthew to ignore.

He said, "We've not moved any yet. We've been rounding up steers. Blake wants all of them shipped back to Three Rivers. So that has to be done before we turn the cows out on the range."

"And after that?"

He finished chewing a bite of tortilla before he spoke. "We'll move certain herds to different areas of the ranch. It all depends on the available grazing." He glanced at her. "We're doing the same job this year that we did last year. You didn't come around or ask questions then."

Shaking her head, she said, "You men have enough to do without a woman showing up and getting in the way. Unless you're talking about Mom, or Vivian, or Isabelle. They all know what they're doing on the back of a horse or in a cow lot. I was never good at any of that."

Her admission surprised him. "You never wanted to learn?"

"I tried, but I usually ended up getting in trouble more than being helpful. Once I dropped my rein, and when I leaned forward to pick it up, my spur hit the flank of the horse. I ended up being bucked off into the fence and got two black eyes from the wild ride. Another time I was helping at the branding fire and somehow got my arm caught between the rope and the calf. I wore a cast for two months after that incident."

"Those things happen all the time in ranch work."

"Yes, but they never happen to Mom or Viv. They're smart enough to avoid trouble."

He leveled a challenging look at her. "So you're afraid to get out among the cows and horses."

Her spine stiffened to a straight line. "I'm not afraid of anything!"

"Hmm. Maureen will be glad to hear that. She thinks you're afraid to come home."

Her chin thrust forward. "I am home. Red Bluff is Hollister range, too, you know."

Yeah, he knew. Just like he knew that she was like a piece of dynamite. Jostle her too much and she might just explode in his face.

"So, what are you afraid of, Matthew?" she tossed the question at him. "Getting burned again by another piece of fluff like Renee?"

Compared to the heat of the day, the kitchen was cool. So why did he feel a sheen of sweat collecting beneath the collar of his shirt?

"I've learned about women since Renee," he said, his gaze fixed firmly on the food in front of him.

He heard her let out a long sigh.

"I've learned about men since Graham, too," she said, then reached over and gave his forearm a gentle squeeze.

"Ouch! Damn!"

She jerked her hand back and stared at him in comical confusion. "Oh! I guess I don't know my own strength. Sorry if I hurt you."

He shook his head. "It's not you—I was in a lot of thorns and cacti today. I think some are still stuck in my arms."

Concern wiped the humor from her face and she quickly rose to her feet. "Finish eating," she instructed. "And don't get up until I get back."

She was bossier than Blake ever thought about being, Matthew thought. But what the hell, giving in was easier than trying to argue with her.

A few minutes later, as he shoveled in the last bite of food from his plate, Camille returned carrying a large straw basket.

She placed it on the table and then, pushing his dirty plate aside, ordered him to roll up his sleeves.

Seeing the basket was full of first aid items, he let out a loud groan.

"No! I don't need doctoring! Forget it!"

Her pretty lips formed a tight line as she stared at him. "I'm not forgetting anything. And I'm not going to hurt you! So quit being a big baby."

"The guys that rode with me today also got thorns and stickers. Are you going to go out to the bunkhouse and treat them, too?" he demanded.

"No. The men in the bunkhouse can help each other. You only have me."

She began to lay out an assortment of cotton swabs, ointment, peroxide and a pair of tweezers. Matthew bit back a groan, and rolled up the sleeves of his denim shirt past his elbows.

"Hell, Camille, you act like I've never been stuck with a thorn before," he muttered. "This happens all the time."

"Maybe it does. But I happen to know that mesquite thorns are poisonous to humans. If you don't get them out and disinfect the spot, it will become infected."

"I know all that. I told the men to be careful."

"Humph. Guess you think your hide is so tough you're immune," she said.

She sat down and reached for the arm nearest to her. Matthew tried to ignore the feel of her hands on his bare flesh, but it was impossible to do, and after a moment, he decided to quit fighting the sensation and simply enjoy it.

Bending her head, she carefully studied the back of his forearm. "This is awful. It's no wonder you yelled when I squeezed your arm. I see three, maybe four thorns still stuck in the flesh."

"We rode through thick brush today."

"Guess you were wearing your chaps." She picked up the tweezers and, after disinfecting them, attempted to pull out one of the longer thorns.

He said, "I don't leave home without them."

"Good thing. Otherwise your legs would be full of these things."

And Matthew couldn't imagine her hands touching his legs. No. That would be more than he could handle.

"This is probably going to hurt," she warned. "I'm going to have to probe with a needle."

"Go ahead. You're a long distance from my heart."

She lifted her head and their gazes locked.

"Really?" she asked. "I never believed you had one of those things."

He had one, all right, Matthew thought. And at the

moment it was banging against his ribs with the desperation of a trapped bird.

"You think I'm a rock—or something?"

Her gaze fell to his lips and for a crazy second he thought she was going to lean forward and kiss him. But his thinking must have been dead wrong because all of a sudden she dropped her gaze back to his arm.

"Or something," she murmured. "Except for Daddy, I always thought you never felt much about anyone or thing."

A hollow sensation spread through his chest and made his voice stilted when he spoke. "Joel was the first man who ever treated me like I was more than a doormat. He taught me that I was just as worthy as the next man and just as capable if I wanted to be. He changed my life."

She stopped the probing and, clasping her hands warmly over his arm, she lifted her gaze to his. "Daddy was special like that. But I— I'm missing something, Matthew. What about the uncle who raised you?"

He grimaced. "I'm surprised you knew about him."

"I don't. I mean, I remember Daddy saying you came from Gila Bend and that an uncle had raised you. That's all I ever knew."

"Odin Waggoner was a bastard and his brother, my father, was no better."

Her eyes were full of questions as she studied his face, and Matthew wanted to tell her that he didn't talk to anyone about his growing-up years. But that wasn't entirely right. He used to talk to Joel about them. Because he knew the big-hearted rancher had understood and never looked down on him for being raised in a dysfunctional family.

"Well, guess you couldn't put your feelings about them any plainer than that."

The questions in her eyes were now shadowed with something like sorrow. That wasn't what Matthew wanted or needed from her.

"No use trying to make something ugly sound pretty. When I was just a little boy, my father would leave for months at a time, to work in the copper mines, or so my mother would say. He supposedly would send money to her to keep me and my older sister fed and clothed and a roof over our heads. But if he did, it was very little. My mother worked cleaning houses for the more well-to-do families around Gila Bend. That's how we actually survived."

Shaking her head, she asked, "How did you end up with your uncle?"

He let out a long sigh. "Well, Mom eventually saw the writing on the wall and divorced Aaron, and not long afterwards, we got word that he'd been killed in a mining accident down in Bisbee. The news hardly caused a ripple through our house. My sister and I could only think that our mother was finally and truly free of the man. But a couple of years later, she developed a blood disease and died. And because my sister and I were still minors, we had to go live with Uncle Odin or be dealt out to foster homes."

"I take it that your uncle wasn't father material," she said quietly.

Matthew snorted. "He had about as much business trying to take care of two young kids as a rattlesnake with a nest full of bird eggs. As soon as Claire and I were old enough, we lit out of there. I wound up in Gila

Bend, and my sister didn't stop until she reached California. She lives in Bishop now."

"Is she married?"

"She was. But it didn't work out. I guess us Waggoners aren't built for marriage."

Something flickered in her eyes, but before he could figure out what she was thinking, her gaze returned to the thorns in his arm.

"So, how did you find your way up to Three Rivers Ranch?"

"It was branding time and Joel had put an ad in the Phoenix newspaper for dayworkers. I took a chance and drove up there. I knew it was a huge, respected ranch and I figured if I could get hired to work for a few days, the reference would help me get hired at a ranch that needed to fill full-time positions."

She continued to probe for the thorn. "After you came to Three Rivers I don't ever remember you leaving."

"No. To this day I'll never know what Joel saw in me. I was young and green with so much to learn."

She glanced up long enough to give him a faint smile. "Guess you did learn. Mom and Blake say they couldn't run the ranch without you."

"They won't have to try. I'd never leave Three Rivers." Renee had tried to pull him away, to drag him to California, where she thought there would be bigger and brighter things for both of them. But even his infatuation for his pretty young wife hadn't been enough to lure him away from the only real home he'd ever known.

"No," she said. "I don't expect you would."

Matthew didn't make any sort of reply, and for the next few minutes Camille concentrated on removing the thorns from his arms. After disinfecting the areas, she began to smooth ointment over the torn skin.

Her fingers were velvety soft, like a butterfly's wings, and he found himself mesmerized by the gentle touch. So much so that he hardly noticed when she rolled down his sleeves and snapped the cuffs back around his wrists.

"There," she said softly. "That should help, but you need to keep an eye on them."

"Thank you, Camille. You're a good nurse."

The smile on her face was a little mysterious and definitely tempting. "I'd rather be called a good cook."

As she started to gather up the medical supplies, Matthew rose to his feet. "All right. You're a good cook, too. Thanks for supper."

"Why don't you go on into the living room and make yourself comfortable. I'll bring you some dessert and coffee."

He didn't need dessert and coffee. Nor did he need to lounge around in her living room like he belonged there. What he needed was to get as much distance as he could from the woman. If he didn't, he was going to end up doing something very stupid. Like kiss her.

"It's getting late. I really should go to bed," he said.

"Tomorrow is Sunday."

"That doesn't change anything for me and the men. We're heading out again at five thirty."

Disappointment caused her features to droop. "Oh. I thought I might talk you into going to church with me. It's a simple nondenominational church over by Dragoon."

Matthew truly would've liked going with her. Attending church with the Hollisters was a routine he'd never broken since he'd gone to work for the family. It gave him a feeling of togetherness and a sense of belonging.

"I'll try to go while I'm here. Maybe next Sunday. Okay?"

He didn't deserve the wide smile she gave him. "Okay. So you go sit. I'll be there in a minute."

She practically shooed him out of the kitchen, and Matthew found his way through a wide arched doorway and into the living room. The long room was mostly dark, with only two small table lamps lighting the area around a red leather couch and matching armchair. Across from the leather furniture, another couch and two armchairs were covered in a brown, nubby-type fabric. At the far end of the room, a TV was playing without the sound. Currently, there was an old Western on the screen. A group of cowboys were riding frantically to turn a stampeding herd of cattle.

As Matthew took a seat on the leather couch, he felt like he'd been run over by a stampeding herd just like the one on the TV screen. The thorn wounds on his arms stung, his shoulders ached from hours of riding, and his eyes burned from lack of sleep and squinting for hours in the fierce sun.

Leaning his head against the back of the couch, he closed his eyes and allowed his body to relax against the soft cushions. Outside he could hear the faint sound of the wind rattling the bougainvillea growing near the window, and farther away, the cattle continued to bawl. Not as loudly as last night, but they were still impatient to be on the open range.

The hypnotic sounds lulled him closer to the edge of sleep. He didn't know Camille was anywhere in the room until he felt her hand cupping the side of his face.

Chapter Four

The contact of Camille's hand against his cheek caused Matthew's eyes to fly open, and he looked around to see she was sitting close to his side, studying him with a mixture of concern and indulgence.

"Uh—sorry—I guess I must've dozed off."

"Yes. I could tell," she said softly. "I should've let you sleep. But I was afraid you'd stay here on the couch all night. And you need to be in bed."

He needed to be in bed, all right, Matthew thought. With her soft body beneath his. The erotic thought was a hopeless one, but he couldn't stop it from entering his mind and lingering there like a haunting dream.

"No need to worry," he said a little gruffly. "I'm awake now."

She dropped her hand and leaned forward toward the long coffee table in front of the couch. Matthew's head had cleared enough for him to see she'd brought a tray with two cups and two bowls. Apparently she was planning to have dessert with him.

"I brought coffee and bread pudding," she said. "I made it at the diner today and the customers seemed to enjoy it. You might like it, too."

She handed him the bowl and cup, and Matthew expected her to take hers to a different chair, or at least scoot a cushion or two down the couch from him. But she didn't. Instead, she remained by his side, so close that her shoulder and thigh were touching his.

Trying to ignore the tempting contact, he asked, "Are you the only cook at the diner?"

"Yes. It's not big enough to need more than one. Although the owner does have a backup in case I'm sick or need to take off for some reason. But that only happens rarely."

He spooned a bite of the pudding into his mouth and very nearly groaned at the delicious taste of cinnamon, raisins and custard-soaked bread. "This is delicious," he said, then shook his head with disbelief. "I'll be honest, Camille, I never thought of you as liking to cook. But apparently you do. I can see you take pride in your work."

"Thank you, Matthew. I do. It makes me happy to create something that gives people joy." She turned an eager look on him. "I'd like for you to come by and see the place before you leave. If you get a chance, that is."

"I'll try."

His half-hearted promise was enough to put a bright smile on her face, and Matthew was suddenly thinking about Blake's remark about Camille needing to get her head on straight. As far as Matthew could see, she had her head on perfectly straight. She wasn't crying, or pining, or miserable, and though the whole family believed she was hiding from life, she seemed to be doing just the opposite.

"I'll tell you a secret, Matthew. I've been having some serious talks with the man who owns the diner. The place is getting busier every day. And I want to expand the menu and start having daily specials. You know, the old-fashioned blue-plate thing—like meat loaf and pinto beans and that sort of home-style food. He's not sure he'd profit over the expense, but I'm sure he would. Since he's been hedging, I decided to offer to buy him out."

That sounded like she'd already made up her mind to stay here in Cochise County permanently, Matthew thought.

"And how did the owner react to your offer?"

"He's thinking on it. Which I understand. He's owned the place for twenty years. But he's talked a lot about retiring so that he and his wife can travel. I'm keeping my fingers crossed that he'll decide to sell."

Matthew scraped the last of the pudding from the bowl, then placed it on the coffee table. "That would be a huge responsibility," he said. "Not to mention the money involved."

"I have enough and more."

She wasn't bragging, simply stating a fact. But then, none of the Hollisters ever bragged about their bank accounts. Maybe about their babies, or a horse or a cow, but never about money.

"I've heard that cafés and restaurants are very risky businesses."

Nodding, she returned her bowl and cup to the tray

on the coffee table. "That's true. But this one is an old establishment. And if the blue plate thing didn't work out, I could always go back to just short orders—like it's always been."

Questions rolled through his mind. "What do you think your family would say about all this? Or have you already mentioned it to them?"

Surprise crossed her face. "Are you kidding? You're the only one I've told. And I hope you'll not say anything—for a while, at least."

Using his thumb and forefinger, he pulled an imaginary zipper in front of his lips. "My lips are sealed."

She grinned. "Thanks," she said. "It's not like I want to keep the idea from them completely. But I'd rather wait—until I see if Norman will decide to sell."

"I'll be honest, Camille, I don't think they'll be happy about your plans."

Shrugging, she glanced away. "No. They won't be happy at all. But that's okay." Turning her gaze back to him, she reached for his hands, and as her fingers curled tightly around his, she said, "Matthew, I need to do what makes me happy. I think you can understand that, don't you?"

"Sure." But did she really know what would make her happy? That's what her mother and siblings would be asking. As for Matthew, he understood that as the baby of the family, she'd had to contend with lots of pampering and sheltering. Too much of it, in fact. "But I'm not the one you need to convince."

Her lips twisted to a wry slant. "I suppose not. But it would make me feel better to hear you say I'm not going around with my head in the clouds."

She wanted his approval. He'd never expected that

from Camille. Maybe because Renee, and the few women he'd dated afterwards, had never seemed to care what he thought about their ideas or plans. All that mattered was their own opinions.

Before he knew what he was doing, his thumbs began to stroke the backs of her hands. "Your head is very much attached to the rest of your body, Camille. And the way I see it, you have a right to dream and hope and plan."

To his dismay, her eyes began to glisten with moisture, and then she leaned forward and pressed her lips against his cheek. "Thank you, Matthew. For being so sweet."

His resistance didn't crumble, it snapped like a dry twig beneath the heel of his boot. And suddenly his hands were in her hair, tugging her face away from his.

"I'm not sweet, Camille," he muttered roughly. "And I don't want to see tears in your eyes. I'd rather see fire! And need!"

She gasped, and then her eyes took on a look of wonder as they searched his face. Matthew's fingers began to move in her hair and in the back of his mind, he could only think how she felt like silk and satin and smelled like a meadow of sweet grass and sunshine.

"Oh, Matthew," she whispered. "Please, kiss me. Please."

Her plea struck something deep inside him, but he didn't take the time to ask himself what the feeling meant. Instead, he jerked her into his arms and wrapped his lips over hers.

There wasn't anything soft, or sweet, or tender about the union of their lips. It was like two winds colliding and merging to create one wild storm. He was so caught up in the hungry search of her lips, he barely heard the tiny moans in her throat or felt her arms curl tightly around his neck.

It wasn't until the two of them had fallen over onto the couch and his upper body was draped over hers that he finally came to his senses. But even then he was slow to pull his lips from hers.

"I—uh—think that turned out to be more than a kiss." His voice sounded like he'd been eating roofing tacks, but she didn't seem to notice. Instead, her hands tightened on the back of his neck and tugged until his mouth was hovering above hers.

"I'm glad that it turned out to be more," she whispered. "Because I want much more than a kiss from you, Matthew."

Just hearing her say such a thing caused a battle of wills to erupt inside him. "You don't know what you're saying."

He started to pull away from her, but she held on tight, until giving in to the tempting call of her lips became a far easier choice than forsaking the warmth of her arms.

This time when he kissed her, he tempered his need and made a slow but thorough exploration of her lips. He'd thought the calm connection would cool the fire racing along his veins, but instead, it was like pouring a slow, steady stream of gas on a simmering blaze.

By the time he managed to straighten himself away from her, a hot ache was gripping his loins and he was sure he'd never be able to get enough oxygen back into his lungs.

"I'm sorry, Camille. But that isn't going to happen." He still sounded hoarse and a hank of hair was stabbing his right eye. He shoved the curl back off his forehead and attempted to clear his throat. "This—whatever this was—should've never happened."

He was expecting her reaction to be angry or, at the very least, offended. But it was neither. Instead, she sat up, and with a soft little smile on her face, she touched fingers to his cheek.

"You don't believe that any more than I do."

He was trying to come up with some sort of response when she suddenly turned away and began gathering the dirty dishes on the coffee table.

Jarred by the sudden switch of her attention, he asked, "What are you doing?"

"Isn't it clear? I'm picking up our mess."

He stared at her in disbelief. Moments ago they'd been on their way to having sex. Now she was cleaning up their dessert dishes as though nothing had happened!

"And that's all you have to say?"

She stood and picked up the tray from the coffee table. "No. I say you're very tired. Go to bed."

Go to bed? For one damned minute he thought about grabbing her hand and leading her straight to the bedroom. The trouble with that notion was that Matthew knew she wouldn't resist. And later, after the fire in his body had cooled, he'd hate himself.

Not bothering to say more, she left the living room.

Matthew watched her go and then, cursing under his breath, he pushed himself off the couch and went straight to his bedroom. But even after he climbed into the queen-sized bed and shut off the lights, he knew it would be hours before he'd be able to sleep.

Sunday was the only day the diner was closed, and Camille usually used the off time to catch up on errands that she couldn't normally do during the week.

After church, she made the twenty-minute drive to Benson and purchased a large supply of groceries before she drove home to Red Bluff. She'd carried everything into the house and was putting the last of the canned goods away when her phone rang.

Seeing it was her mother, Camille carried the phone out to the courtyard and made herself comfortable on a chaise lounge.

"Hi, Mom. What's up?"

"Hello, honey! We just finished Sunday dinner and I thought I'd call to check on you."

The last of October meant winter was coming for most people, but the sun was still exceptionally warm in southern Arizona, and Camille loved the feel of it sinking into her skin and warming her face.

"I'm doing great. What about you?"

Camille could hear her mother's sigh. It was full of weariness or sadness. She wasn't exactly sure which, but she did know they were sounds that weren't normally made by her mother.

"I'm okay. We've been very busy up here—moving all the cattle down from the Prescott range. Snow has already hit Flagstaff. We don't want to take any chances with the cow/calf pairs being caught in a snowstorm."

Camille could've reminded her mother that there was no need for her to spend hours of the day in the saddle, doing a job that was tiring, even for a man. But she'd be wasting her breath. Maureen loved to be outside, riding and working with the cattle. It was something she'd done all her life and it had especially bonded her with Joel during the years of their long marriage.

"Do you have them all moved?" Camille asked.

"No. We're heading back up there in the morning. Tomorrow should wrap it up, though."

"It's hot down here," Camille said. "I don't look for it to cool much until Christmas."

There was a long pause, and then Maureen said, "I don't suppose you've thought much about coming home for the holidays."

"No. I wouldn't dream of leaving Norman at such a busy time at the diner."

"But it doesn't bother you to neglect your family during Thanksgiving and Christmas." She let out another long sigh. "Camille, there are times I just don't understand you. If you're worried that people around here are still talking about Graham Danby jilting you, then you're wrong."

Camille let out an unladylike curse. "Mom, I've told you a hundred times or more. The guy means nothing to me. He did me a giant favor when he asked for his ring back. I'm happier now than I ever have been. And if I saw Graham today, I'd thank him for having more sense than I did. He knew we didn't belong together— it just took me a while to see that."

Maureen snorted. "That would be easy to believe if I hadn't seen all those tears you shed when you were packing your bags and leaving Three Rivers. You were crushed."

"No, Mom. *I* wasn't crushed. Only my pride," Camille assured her, then said, "You know, you and my brothers and sisters are all welcome to come down here and spend the holidays at Red Bluff. I think there would be plenty of room, even with all the babies."

"Ha! It would take a caravan to move us all down there. But I might take you up on the invitation—at least for a few days. The boys have really been getting on my nerves."

Camille frowned. It wasn't like her mother to complain about her sons for any reason. Especially now that all of them had settled down with their own families. "What are my brothers doing to get on your nerves?"

"Hovering over me like they expect me to fall apart any minute. I may not look like I did ten years ago, but I'm hardly ready to sit in a rocker!"

"Give them a break, Mom. Now that they all have wives, I think they're just more aware of how hard you work."

"Maybe. But I don't believe that's the cause of their behavior. Especially Joe. He thinks I'm having some sort of PTSD over Joel's death. And none of them appreciate the fact that I've told them to let the whole incident go. They're all like terriers digging beneath a chain link fence. They refuse to give up until they've reached some sort of conclusion." She heaved out a heavy breath. Then, after a brief pause, she said, "Sorry, Camille. You don't want to hear this. And I don't want to talk about it. So tell me, how's it going with Matthew?"

Camille sat straight up. "Matthew?"

"Yes. Our foreman," she answered drolly. "Blake tells me he's staying there in the house with you. But I don't guess you see him that much. I know how busy the men stay when they're moving cattle down there."

"Oh, well—I see him when he comes in at night. I've been feeding him and uh—making sure he has everything he needs."

"That's good. I was hoping you'd be nice to him."

Camille frowned. "Mom, did you honestly believe I wouldn't be nice?"

"Oh, I don't know. I always got the impression that he rubbed you the wrong way."

Except for those hot kisses last night, he'd never

rubbed her in any way. That was the problem. Funny how it had taken Camille years to figure that out.

In the most innocent tone she could manage, she said, "I can't imagine where you got that idea."

"Well, you practically laughed with glee when he and Renee divorced."

"That's because she was horrible for him," Camille reasoned. "And Matthew should have realized she was a horrible fit for him."

"Uh-huh. You mean like you should've seen how Graham was all wrong for you?" Maureen asked smugly.

"Exactly," Camille retorted, then sighed as images of last night whirled through her mind. "Actually, Mom, I'm—enjoying Matthew. He's a lot different than the way I remembered."

"Different? In what way?"

Instead of a spindly young guy, who'd been totally unsure of himself, Matthew had turned into a sexy hunk of confident man, she thought. To her mother, she said, "Well, he was always sort of quiet. That hasn't changed much. But I'm learning he has a bit of a sense of humor and he's a good listener." Pausing, she chuckled. "Or he might just be letting me talk so he won't have to."

Several seconds of silence passed and just when Camille was wondering what her mother was thinking, Maureen said, "I'm glad you're enjoying him, honey. I don't have to tell you how much Matthew means to the family. And he's—well, I'm not sure he's ever gotten over his difficult childhood."

The things Matthew had told her about his family, or lack of one, were still haunting Camille, and she wondered how he'd grown up to be such a responsible man. If asked, he'd probably give all the credit to Joel, but that wouldn't be entirely right. He'd been a hardworking, trustworthy man when he'd first come to Three Rivers. Joel had simply nourished the goodness in him.

Camille said, "Last night he mentioned having a sister. I wasn't aware that he had a sibling. I've never heard any of you mention her. Does he ever see her?"

"Not often. The last time was right after you left for Red Bluff. Blake purchased a bull over in California and he sent Matthew to haul him home. The trip gave Matthew a chance to stop by Claire's place."

"I see." Deciding she'd better change the subject before her mother started to think her interest in Matthew was a bit excessive, she said, "I guess you're going to have a Halloween party. Do all the kids have their costumes yet?"

Maureen chuckled. "Abagail and Andrew are going to be cats with tails and whiskers. That's the most important thing, of course."

"How cute," Camille said with a laugh. "What about Nick and Hannah? They probably think they're too old to party with the babies."

"Not in the least. Nick and Hannah love being big bosses of their little siblings. And anyway, Viv has promised to take those two to a party on the res that's just for teens and tweens."

Missing out on spending time with her nieces and nephews was the one regret Camille often had about making her home here on Red Bluff. On the other hand, it would be difficult living back on Three Rivers and her being the only Hollister sibling without a spouse or a child. It was hard enough to deal with living two hundred fifty miles away.

Single and childless at the age of twenty-eight was not the way Camille had envisioned or hoped her life would be. But it had turned out that way and now she was determined not to lament the situation, but embrace her independence. As far as she was concerned that was far better than nursing a broken heart.

"Have you seen Emily-Ann lately?" Camille asked.

"No. But Katherine sees her regularly. She misses you. I know that much."

Emily-Ann had been Camille's best friend since their days in grade school. She ran Conchita's, a tiny coffee shop in Wickenburg that served bakery treats and specialty coffees. "I miss her, too. I'm hoping she can come down for a visit soon."

"Emily-Ann isn't exactly flush with money," Maureen pointed out. "I doubt she can afford to stay away from her job for more than a day or two."

Camille's friend was dependable and hard working. She'd be great as a waitress for the diner. But in spite of the struggles and stigma she'd suffered through, Emily-Ann would never move away from Wickenburg. It was her home.

"I'd make sure she wouldn't have to spend a dime, Mom."

"I expected you to say that. So why don't you invite her down for Thanksgiving?" Maureen suggested. "You could take her to Tucson and do some Christmas shopping."

"That's a nice idea."

"Good. I—"

Her mother's words were suddenly interrupted by the sound of distant voices.

Camille asked, "Mom, do you need to get off the phone?"

"Uh—yes, I'm afraid I do. Blake needs me for something. Love you. And be sure and take extra good care of Matthew."

"Yes—I will. And I love you, too."

Camille punched the phone to disconnect the call, then rose from the lounge chair. As she walked back to the house, her mother's words played over in her mind.

Take extra good care of Matthew.

What would Maureen think if she knew just how much Camille wanted to care for Matthew? Would she think her daughter was reaching for something she could never have? Last night, when he'd kissed her, she'd thought he was finally going to lower the barriers he'd erected between them. For those few brief moments he'd held nothing back and she'd met the reckless desperation of his lips with the same hungry need.

She'd never wanted any man to make love to her as much as she'd wanted Matthew at that moment. But he'd pulled away and implied that their kisses had been a mistake. Could he be right?

As Camille went to her bedroom and changed out of her church clothes, the question continued to circle through her thoughts. For the past two years she'd done a lot of growing, and now it was easy to see where and why she'd made the mistake in getting engaged to Graham. Yes, she'd learned her lesson. But what about now? What about Matthew?

Oh Lord, never in her wildest dreams had she thought his time here at Red Bluff would mean anything more than having a visitor in the house. She'd honestly expected him to be sullen and curt and she'd planned to ignore him as best she could.

How laughable was that? she asked herself as she pulled on jeans and a thin pink shirt. The moment she'd looked across the threshold at Matthew's tired face, something had smacked her right between the breasts. And try as she might, she couldn't get rid of the feeling.

But he wasn't down here for romance, she reasoned with herself. Besides, he'd been divorced and single for nearly ten years. The man clearly had no desire to marry again. So what good would it do her to have a brief affair with him? No good. Matthew was right and she knew it. But for some reason her heart wasn't listening to reason.

Chapter Five

After searching the southernmost range of the ranch for the entire day, Matthew and the small crew of cowhands helping him came up with six of the missing ten steers. Although the men were disappointed that they'd not found the last four, Matthew was pleased with the effort. They could've just as easily ended up with zilch for the day.

"When are we going to vaccinate and tag the new cattle, Matthew?" Pate asked, as he steered the double-seated work truck coupled to a long stock trailer over the rough ground.

Slumped in the passenger seat, Matthew was attempting to grab a bit of shut-eye during the drive back to the ranch yard, but with Pate hitting every rock in the old roadbed, his head was banging around like a punching bag.

Biting back a tired groan, he straightened on the worn leather seat and gazed out the window at the desert hills covered with purple twilight. Red Bluff was an enchanting place and not just because Camille was here, he decided. There were parts of the ranch that were incredibly green to be located in such a desert area. Then there were other parts that were full of high rocky bluffs and hundreds of tall saguaros with their arms reaching toward the wide, endless sky.

He wondered how much, if any, of this land Camille ever seen. Did any of it truly matter to her? Or did she only care about the house and having her privacy? Last night, when she'd talked about trying to help out with the ranching chores at Three Rivers, he'd gotten the impression that she'd wanted to be as much of a cowgirl as her mother and sister, but she lacked the confidence to keep trying.

Last night. Oh Lord, he wished he could quit thinking about last night. He wished he could block out every scent, every taste and touch his brain cells had gathered when he and Camille had kissed so passionately. If he lived to be a hundred, the memory would still be enough to curl his toes.

"Don't you think we ought to be letting some of the other cattle loose?" Pate continued to throw questions at him. "Curly and Abel have already poured out tons of feed and hay."

Since Pate had the least experience of all the men here and was constantly peppering him with questions, Matthew tried to hold on to his patience and remember how it was to be green and uncertain.

"And they'll keep pouring out more tons until we

have everything ready," Matthew explained. "That includes finding the last four steers."

"Pate, why are you concerned about the feed and hay?" Scott asked from the back seat. "You're not paying for it out of your paycheck."

Looking over his shoulder, Pate smirked at the other ranch hand. "No. But I'm riding for the brand. I don't want Three Rivers to spend money unnecessarily."

TooTall grunted. "No need to worry. We'll find the four steers tomorrow. Right, Matthew?"

TooTall was always positive and a man of few words. More often than not, he called Matthew Yellow Hair. But tonight he'd used his given name, and the sound of it put a wry smile on Matthew's lips.

"You're always right, TooTall. And I don't know what I'd do without your level head around."

Scooting to the edge of the seat, TooTall poked his face between the bucket seats. "Does that mean you're gonna let me stay down here on Red Bluff and work with you?"

Completely bewildered by TooTall's question, Matthew twisted around to look at him. "What are you talking about? We'll be going back to Three Rivers in a couple of weeks, or less."

"Yes. But you'll be coming back."

"Not until next winter."

TooTall shook his head. "No. You'll be coming back sooner. And then you'll stay."

TooTall had always been the mystical sort. But even for him, this prediction was far out in left field.

Tired as he was, Matthew had to laugh. "You're way off base, TooTall. I won't have any reason to come back here to Red Bluff, unless Blake wants me to come with him just for a look around."

His expression completely serious, TooTall shook his head. "You're wrong, Matthew. So do I get to come with you and be your right-hand man? Your ramrod?"

Matthew couldn't think of any other man he'd rather have as his right-hand man. So, not to hurt his feelings, he said, "Okay, TooTall, if your prediction comes true, you'll be my ramrod."

"You promise?"

"I'll put it down in writing," Matthew assured him.

"No. You cross your heart, Yellow Hair. That's better."

Seeing that the cowboy was truly serious, Matthew complied by making an X mark across his heart. "Okay. Does that make you happy?"

"I'm happy," TooTall told him.

Behind the steering wheel, Pate guffawed. "What a crock of crap. He's been chewing agave!"

Matthew cut the young man a steely glare. "What the hell are you laughing at? No one has been chewing agave—unless it's you! And if I ever catch you doing it, I'll kick your ass all the way back to the ranch yard. Got that?"

Pate's expression sobered instantly. "Yes. I got it."

A half hour later, Pate parked the truck and trailer near the big red barn, and the four men climbed out and went to work unloading the steers and the horses. Once they had all the livestock settled for the night and their tack and gear stored away, Matthew started to the house, only to have his phone start ringing.

Seeing it was Blake, he answered, but the signal was too weak for the man's voice to come through clearly.

Matthew hung up and walked on to the house. When he reached the inner courtyard, he sat down on a padded lounge chair and tried to return Blake's call.

"Blake, can you hear me?"

"Clear as a bell now," Blake answered. "I was just calling to see how things are going down there."

"We're making progress," he told him. "No problems. I figure we can ship the steers up day after tomorrow. TooTall predicts we'll find the last four tomorrow."

Blake grunted with amusement. "And TooTall's predictions always come true."

Matthew wasn't about to bring up the man's other prediction. It was far too strange and frankly unnerving to repeat out loud.

"I'll have a man ready to come after the steers," Blake assured him. "Is there anything else you need? Is the feed and hay holding steady?"

"We're okay there."

"And the water? I don't suppose you've had a chance to check the wells yet?"

Matthew wiped a weary hand over his face. "No. But we'll get to it."

Blake cursed under his breath. "I should've sent at least two more men with you, Matthew. There's too much to do down there and you don't have near enough help. I don't want you collapsing on me."

"Hell, Blake, I'm not going to collapse. Everything will come together. Don't worry about any of it."

The other man let out a long breath. "Both ranches are growing and Holt keeps telling me that more cattle means more men. I think my brother is right."

Matthew massaged his closed eyelids. His mouth felt like he'd been eating dirt and his eyes had been scraped with sandpaper. "Are you thinking about running cattle down here all year round? I'm talking about more than just a few steers?"

"Funny you should ask that. Mom and I have been tossing the idea around. It would mean investing a lot of money. But we think it would pay off. Why are you asking?"

Because TooTall was making strange prophecies, Matthew could've told him. Aloud, he said, "With you buying the five hundred extra head, it crossed my mind."

"Hmm. What do you think about the idea? And don't be afraid to speak frankly, Matthew. I always value your opinion, whether I agree with it or not."

"Well, I don't think I've ever covered this whole ranch. Not on horseback or in a vehicle. At least, not for several years—since Joel was still with us. I couldn't say how many cattle this land is capable of supporting until I had a good look at all of it."

Blake went silent for a moment and then he said, "You know, you've given me an idea. And before you start cursing a blue streak, just hear me out. Once you get the cattle settled, I'd like for you to take a few extra days to really look the place over. I hate to admit that it's been years since I've seen much of it myself. And since you're already down there, it would be the perfect opportunity."

Hell, no! He wasn't going to stay down here any longer than he had to. Even though the thought was racing through his head, Matthew didn't say it to Blake. He'd wait a few days, after things were smoothing out here, before he began to curse that blue streak at his boss.

"You don't need for me to do it," Matthew hedged.

"Any of the men can have a look around and give you a report."

Blake let out a loud laugh. "Sure, Matthew. Like I could trust just anyone's judgment. Why do you think you're the foreman of Three Rivers? Because of your good looks?"

Matthew snorted. "Not hardly."

"Damn right, not hardly. It's because you have an eagle eye and a rancher's mind. But we'll talk about this later. Right now Kat is helping the twins try on their cat suits and they want me to come watch."

"Cat suits?"

Blake laughed and Matthew realized that in spite of the heavy load the eldest Hollister brother carried, he was a happy man now that he had Katherine and the children in his life.

"Yes. You know. Meow! Thursday night is Halloween and Mom's throwing one of her big parties. The kids can't wait. Sorry you can't be here, buddy. I'll eat some candy just for you."

"Thanks, Blake. But I really think I'd rather have Holt drink a bourbon and Coke for me."

Blake laughed loudly. "I'll tell him. I'm sure he'll be more than happy to do that little thing for you. Talk to you later, Matthew."

Blake cut the connection, and Matthew dropped the phone back into his shirt pocket, but he didn't immediately leave his seat on the lounge. His head was whirling and he needed a minute in the quiet before he walked into the house and faced Camille again.

Who are you kidding, Matthew? You're not worried about facing Camille again. Your insides are tied into knots with worry about how you're going to keep your

*hands off her, when every cell in your body is aching
to make love to her.*

Cursing at the damning voice in his head, he lifted
his hat from his head and raked a hand through his
hair. He was hot and dirty and sweat had dried to salty
patches on the front and back of his shirt. Thank goodness he and the men had gotten in early enough tonight
that he had time for a shower before he ate.

"There you are. I thought I heard someone out here
talking."

Camille's voice startled him, and he jerked his head
around to see her walking up the stone pathway to
where he was sitting. She was wearing jeans and cowboy boots, and the front tails of her shirt were knotted
at her waist. The clothes suited her, but it was the smile
on her face that transformed her into an enchantress.

"I had a call from Blake," he explained.

"Oh. I hope you told him hello for me."

"No. I didn't. I will next time."

She sat down next to him on the lounge and he was
suddenly assaulted with her sunny scent and the feel of
her soft, warm shoulder pressing against his.

"Blake is annoyed with me because I'm down here
instead of up there," she said. "He blames me for Mom's
state of mind."

"Not completely."

"Humph. You don't have to handle me with kid
gloves, Matthew. Anyway, I've got news for Blake.
Mom might like for me to move back to Three Rivers,
but what's really aggravating her is that her sons are
ignoring her wishes."

He studied her from the corner of his eye. "You're
talking about the investigation into Joel's death now."

"Right."

Matthew wasn't sure how much Blake, Holt, Chandler, or Joseph had told Camille about the information they'd discovered a few months back. Initially, when Joseph had learned that Joel had been spotted with a woman at the Phoenix livestock sale barn before his death, the brothers had decided to keep the information to themselves, their reason being that none of them wanted their sisters hurt by the idea that Joel might have been cheating on Maureen. But they could've changed their minds and let their sisters in on the development. Either way, Matthew wasn't going to repeat something to Camille that might ultimately hurt her and anger her brothers.

"I wouldn't dwell on it, Camille. Your mother is hardly falling apart. She's too strong for that."

"I wish my brothers viewed everything as sensibly as you do."

He shook his head. "It's always easier to see the whole picture when you're standing on the outside looking in. It's when a guy gets too close to something that he has trouble seeing everything."

Even though he wasn't looking at her directly, he could feel her gaze drop to his lips. He was trying to decide whether he should jump to his feet and leave the lounge, or jerk her into his arms, when she suddenly reached over and wrapped a thumb and forefinger around his chin.

"I'm close," she murmured as she steered his face toward hers. "So what are you seeing?"

He needed to draw in a deep, cleansing breath, but his brain wasn't communicating with his lungs. It was too busy thinking about having her lips next to his.

"I'm seeing a little vixen that's asking for more trouble than she could possibly know."

Her fingers moved to his cheek. "Yes," she whispered. "But it's worth the risk. Don't you think?"

Even though it was dark, the footlights edging the stone floor of the porch were enough to reveal the inviting look in her eyes, and Matthew decided he was tired of fighting her and this unbearable need to have her in his arms.

"Worth the risk and more," he muttered. Then, clamping his hands at the back of her head, he drew her face up to his. "And right now I don't care if this makes the roof fall in on us."

"Mmm. We don't have a roof over us. Just the open sky—and the stars and—"

"This," he murmured against her lips.

Instantly, she deepened the contact by opening her mouth and wrapping her arms around his neck.

Matthew had never been shot out of a cannon, but he figured this was darned close to it. Like a lighted match landing on a dry tumbleweed, fire exploded inside of him, catapulting him into a dark, dreamy space. Unable to stop the flight, he mindlessly pushed her upper body down on the lounge chair and draped himself over her.

The exotic taste of her kiss intoxicated what was left of his senses, and when he felt her tongue probing for an entryway into his mouth, he gladly gave it to her, all the while knowing he wouldn't be satisfied until he had more and more.

His hands cupped her breasts and as he kneaded their fullness, he imagined his mouth on the softness, his teeth sinking into the budded centers. Above the roaring blood in his ears, he heard her moan, and then he felt her hands working their way to the snaps of his shirt. The moment her hands found enough space to slip inside the fabric and flatten against his skin, he tore his mouth from hers and sucked in a fierce breath.

"I—uh, think we'd better stop this—and go inside."

Her eyes half-closed, she smiled like a contented cat. "Why? The night air feels like cool velvet and you feel even better."

Groaning, he brought his face back to hers and nuzzled his lips against her cheek. "I'm dirty and smell like—"

"Like a real man," she finished before he could. Her fingertips rubbed against the stubble on his jaw. "I like the whiskers and the dust and the sweat. I like—everything about you, Matthew."

"You're crazy. But I'm beginning not to care."

As soon as he said the words, his lips moved back to hers, and as their kiss deepened, Matthew had one thing on his mind. Getting her off the chair and into his bed.

And then the quietness in the courtyard was suddenly interrupted by the distant sound of men's voices shouting back and forth.

Matthew desperately wanted to ignore the commotion, but the responsibilities attached to his job were deeply ingrained in him and he slowly lifted his head and pushed himself to his feet.

"Something is happening at the barn. I hear the men yelling."

Frowning, she sat up and listened along with him.

"Damn it, don't push her leg that way!" Curly shouted loud enough for the sound to carry all the way to the courtyard. "Abel, go get a lariat! We'll pull her out!"

Snapping his shirt back together, Matthew cast Camille a rueful glance. "I have to go."

She jumped to her feet. "Of course you do. I'll see you when you get back."

Matthew hurried out of the courtyard and as his long strides carried him to the barn, he decided he'd either made a great escape, or lost the chance of a lifetime.

Chapter Six

More than an hour later, after Matthew had left to go to the ranch yard, Camille was upstairs in her bedroom when she heard him return to the house. The sound of his movements below was enough to cause her heart to trip all over itself, and with trembling fingers she hurriedly finished pinning her hair into a messy bun.

She didn't know why she'd bothered to change into a long dress and sandals or pin up her hair. If Matthew really wanted to make love to her, it wouldn't matter what she was wearing or how she looked, she thought.

But it mattered to her. Ever since Graham had thrown her over for Crystal Thompson, she'd harbored all kinds of doubts about herself. If she'd not been pretty enough, or woman enough, to keep her fiancé from falling for another woman, then how did she expect to hold on to any man? Especially one like Matthew, who was sexy enough to have women throwing themselves at him.

Isn't that what you're doing, Camille? You know good and darn well that you've been throwing yourself at Matthew from the moment he arrived on the ranch. What has come over you anyway? You've never behaved this way in your entire life. And to make matters worse, you've been vowing to stay celibate and unattached. Now you're trying your best to veer way off course! You're going to get your heart broken, you little ninny, and when you do, you'll have nowhere else to run. No place to hide your wounds.

The sardonic voice going off in her head caused her lips to compress into a thin line. So what if she was the one doing all the pursuing? What was wrong with that? Her father had always taught her to be strong and go after the things she wanted in life. And Lord help her, she wanted Matthew with every fiber of her being.

With that thought in mind, she fastened a pair of golden hoops to her ears and hurried downstairs to the kitchen.

"What was happening down at the barn?" Camille asked as she carried a platter filled with pot roast and vegetables over to the table. "I hope nothing serious."

"Everything is okay now," he assured her. "A cow managed to get her leg stuck through one of the fencing panels. If Curly hadn't happened to go outside and find her in the predicament, she would've probably broken her leg trying to get herself loose. And you know what that would've meant."

"Yes," she said ruefully. "You would've had to put her down. Does she have a calf?"

"Yes. Probably no more than two weeks old. It would've had to be bottle-fed. Which is quite a time-consuming job. But thank God, the mama is okay and so is her calf."

She went back to the cabinet counter to collect a bowl of brown gravy and a basket of hot rolls. As she placed them next to the roast, she said, "I've heard people make stupid comments about ranching life. Like all you have to do is put a few cows on some grass and let them multiply. They couldn't be more wrong. It's a very hard job and many times, heartbreaking."

"You say that like you know firsthand."

"I wasn't just a klutz around the horses and cows, but I was a big softie. I couldn't bear seeing any of the animals sick or injured. Once a cow had twins and I was so excited over them. Daddy gave me the job of giving them bottle milk to help supplement what the mother was able to provide her two babies." She paused and shook her head. "But the weaker of the two calves eventually died and I was totally devastated. I cried for a month over it and after that I refused to go to the barn. I know that was childish of me. But it hurt too much."

"There are a lot of things about ranching that can be brutal," he said. "But the rewarding parts balance it all out."

She gestured to the table. "That's everything," she said. "Let's eat."

He pulled out a chair for her and she thanked him as she took a seat and he pushed forward.

As he sat in the chair angled to her left, he said, "I wasn't expecting you to be eating with me this evening. You didn't have to wait, you know."

She smiled at him. "It's nice not to have to eat alone. And I didn't mind the wait."

They filled their plates and as they began to eat, she

glanced at his arms, which were covered with a long-sleeved white shirt.

"Did you get back into the mesquite and chaparral today?"

"Yes. The area of the ranch where we've been riding is rough and full of brush. But I tried to get them out when I took a shower."

"I'll have a look after we eat."

He didn't say anything, but the look he slanted her spoke volumes. Like if she touched him he wouldn't be responsible for his actions. The idea caused Camille to tremble inside.

After a few moments passed, she asked, "Are you still living in the old foreman's house up on the ridge?"

"Yes. Why?"

She shrugged. "I just wondered, that's all. It's been a while since I left Three Rivers. Some things have changed since then." She laughed lightly, then shook her head. "Let me rephrase that. Many things have changed since then. The house is full of babies and wives. Blake married Katherine and together they have Nick, Abagail and Andrew. Then Chandler married Roslyn and they have little Evelyn."

"You've left out your other siblings," Matthew said. "Joseph married Tessa and they have Little Joe and baby daughter, Spring. Vivian married Sawyer and now, along with Hannah, they have twins, Jacob and Johnny. And Holt and Isabelle will be having their first baby soon. It's been a very productive few years for your family."

Her lips twisted to a wry slant. "My siblings have always been high achievers. Blake manages Three Rivers, Chandler is a veterinarian and owns a very successful clinic. Joseph is deputy sheriff for Yavapai County, Holt is a prestigious horse trainer, and Vivian is an experienced park ranger. And what is little Camille? She's a short order cook in a desert diner. I take everything back I said about my brothers. I'm the reason Mom is depressed."

"Stop it," he ordered. "The poor, pitiful me act doesn't suit you."

She straightened her shoulders. "No. You're right. It doesn't. But sometimes I think—"

"You think too much," he interrupted. "About the wrong things. You've already said that being a cook makes you happy. If that's the case, then you should be proud of yourself and proud of your job."

She nodded glumly. Then, after a moment's thought, she nodded with more enthusiasm. "You're right. I could go dig out my college degree and hang it on the wall. I could even go to Tucson and get an office job with an impressive title attached to it. But I'd hate every minute of it. Just like you'd hate it if you had to take over Blake's job and sit behind a desk for most of the day. You'd be a big shot, but would it be worth it?"

"Not to me. I don't want to be a big shot. I'd rather be a saddle bum."

He grinned as he said the last word and Camille laughed. Then, unable to stop herself, she reached over and squeezed his hand.

"I'm so glad that you're here, Matthew. You make me feel good."

His expression suddenly sobered and the regret she saw in his gray eyes was worse than being cut with a knife.

"Camille, I—about what happened out there in the courtyard—I—"

She quickly interrupted, "I don't want to talk about that now, Matthew. Let's just enjoy our food. And—talk about other things. Tell me about Blue Stallion Ranch and this dream ranch that Holt and Isabelle are building together."

For a moment she thought he was going to ignore her plea and begin a long tirade about how they should keep some sensible distance between them. But to her relief he relented and said, "It's on the old Landry Ranch. Just north of Three Rivers. Remember it?"

"Yes. Vaguely. I went over there with Daddy once. It was very pretty over there. Do you think Holt likes being away from Three Rivers?"

"Well, it's not like he's away entirely. He works at Three Rivers on weekdays. His nights and weekends are spent at Blue Stallion. And yes, he's very happy."

Camille thoughtfully shook her head. "Amazing, really. Wild Holt finally under a bit and bridle and with a baby on the way, too. I would've never dreamed it. But I guess the old saying that nothing stays the same is true."

"Yes," he said softly. "Look at you."

"Yeah," she said with a twinge of cynicism. "Look at me."

Another span of silence passed before Matthew spoke again. Even though she'd cut him off when he'd brought up their encounter in the courtyard, Camille couldn't help but wonder what he'd been about to say. That he didn't want to get involved with her? That no matter how much she tempted or taunted, he wasn't going to make love to her?

Just as she let out a long sigh, he asked, "Has Maureen mentioned anything to you about Sam?"

She arched her brows at him. "You mean Sam Leman? Tessa and Joseph's ranch foreman?"

Sam was a crusty cowboy somewhere in his seventies. For years he'd worked for the late Sheriff Ray Maddox until Ray had passed away and Tessa had inherited the Bar X.

He nodded. "Yes, that Sam."

"No. Why? I hope nothing is wrong with him. I always thought he was a charming old guy."

Matthew slanted her a wry look. "All the women do. Especially Isabelle's mother, Gabby. Seems as though a romance has sparked between the two."

Camille's mouth fell open. "Isabelle's mother? I saw her in a few of the photos of Holt and Isabelle's wedding that Mom sent to me. Gabby is a very attractive blonde and quite a bit younger than Sam, isn't she?"

He sipped from his glass of iced tea before he spoke. "I have no idea what Holt's mother-in-law's age actually is, but I'd say she's at least twenty years younger than Sam."

"Wow! Sam is an old desert cowboy who loves horses and goats and bourbon, but he obviously still has what it takes! Wonder how those two got together?"

"Gabby's an artist and it seems she was so taken with the character in Sam's face that she wanted to do a portrait of him. You can imagine how shocked everyone was when Sam agreed to sit for her. The way things have turned out, Sam must've been doing more than just sitting. And Gabby more than painting."

Camille cast him a suggestive smile. "So Gabby is still living back here in Arizona?"

He nodded. "On Blue Stallion Ranch with Isabelle and Holt. But your brother says Sam and Gabby are planning to marry soon. They want to be together while he's still young. That's the way Gabby puts it."

A bittersweet pain squeezed her heart. Would any man ever feel that way about her? To love her so much he didn't want to miss a day, an hour, or a minute without her in his life? Maureen had been blessed with that kind of love. Now Vivian had it with Sawyer. But Camille was beginning to doubt she would ever be the recipient of that kind of devoted emotion.

"That's so romantic," she said huskily.

He leveled a meaningful, knowing look at her. "I expected that kind of response from you. Maureen says the same thing. She gets all teary-eyed whenever she talks about the two of them."

Camille's throat was so tight that she forced herself to swallow a few bites of food before she replied. "Well, Sam has been a friend of the family for as long as I can remember. I'm sure she's happy for him. And—maybe a little sad for herself. You know—losing Daddy like she did."

"Maureen deserves some happiness."

From the corner of her eye, Camille thoughtfully watched him slice into the roast beef on his plate. She said, "Viv tells me that Holt and Chandler have the idea that Mom has fallen in love with someone. Do you believe that?"

"Joel has been gone for a long time. And your mother is human." He glanced at her. "You wouldn't oppose her having a man in her life, would you?"

"No. I want her to be happy. That's all I want."

He fell silent after that, and Camille decided all their

talk about family and romance had left him uncomfortable. Well, she could tell him that just sitting across the table from him unnerved her. But he probably already knew that, she thought. She'd made her desire for him clear enough.

Camille had never pursued a man in her life. Even Graham had been the one to seek her out, and she'd been unable to resist his sweet talk and promises of the kind of future she'd always wanted. It hadn't even mattered that he'd liked the fact that she was an office manager and had wanted her to continue the job after they were married. And when he'd insisted they would make their home in Phoenix, she'd gone along like a helpless calf being dragged to the branding fire.

She'd been so foolish and weak-willed back then, she thought. She'd let Graham define who she was and what she was. But never again. She'd emerged from their broken engagement a different and stronger woman. And this time around she wasn't going to give up, or give in.

Every bite of food was gone from Matthew's plate when he finally rose from the table and carried it and his glass over to the sink. Behind him, he could hear Camille leave the table, and he turned just as she came to stand next to him.

"Thanks for supper, Camille. It was delicious."

"I have apple pie," she told him. "I'll get the coffee going."

"No," he blurted. Then, seeing the confused frown on her face, he added, "I—uh—the pie can wait. I want to talk with you first."

Her expression stoic, she stacked her plate on top of

his. "If you're going to start in about us kissing in the courtyard—"

"That was more than kissing, Camille, and you know it," he stated flatly.

As her blue gaze probed his face, her chin tilted upward. "What if it was more? Don't try to tell me you weren't enjoying it."

Frustration pushed a groan past his throat. "Hell, Camille, what do you think I am? Made of steel?"

"I'm not sure," she said quietly. "Just when I start to think you're human, you want to put a cold wall between us."

Cold? Everything was about her was burning him up, even the part of his brain that was supposed to be holding on to his common sense.

"I'm trying to stop a shipwreck, Camille. We can't just—"

"What? Make love?" As she asked the questions, she moved close enough to slide her palms up the middle of his chest. "Why can't we? We're both adults and unattached."

His nostrils flared at the simple image she was painting. She made it sound so easy and right. And maybe that was the way it should be, he pondered. Maybe he was making too damned much of everything. Maybe he needed to forget about her last name and start thinking of her as the woman he wanted. "You think that's all there is to it?"

Sliding her arms up and around his neck, she arched the front of her body into his. The warm curves pressing into his flesh were impossible to ignore, and with a will of their own, his arms wrapped around her waist and anchored her tightly against him.

"I think you're afraid to admit that you want me," she said softly. "And I don't understand why."

"I'll be gone from here in a few days." Strange how that fact was beginning to weigh on him. Any other time he'd be looking forward to heading home to Three Rivers.

"That's more good reason why we shouldn't waste this time, Matthew."

Like Gabby and Sam, he thought. The couple wanted to make the most of the years they had left. But they were different, he mentally argued. They were in love.

Love. Like hell, Matthew thought cynically. If he waited on love to find him, he'd be living the rest of his life like a monk. This thing he felt for Camille was pure, hot lust and that's all it ever would be.

He looked down at her and as their eyes met, he felt the tight grip he had on his self-control snap. Relief flooded through him, followed by a rampant wave of desire.

"Time. No," he murmured. "We don't have enough."

Deliberately pushing any more thought from his mind, he lowered his mouth to hers.

His sign of surrender must have pleased her because her lips were suddenly moving against his in a way that was both tender and enticing. No woman had ever kissed him like this. Like he was precious and something to cherish. Matthew realized he didn't want it to end. He didn't want this connection with her to end.

When the need for air finally parted their lips, Camille buried her cheek against his chest. "Oh, Matthew, this isn't wrong."

He groaned as his hands roamed her back. "Even if it's wrong I can't fight you anymore."

Lifting her head, she touched her fingertips to his cheek, and in that instant, fear slashed through him. This wasn't the way she was supposed to be looking at him, or touching him. And the middle of his chest wasn't supposed to feel like warm mush.

"I don't want you to fight anything," she whispered. Then, taking his hand, she led him out of the kitchen.

With her hand wrapped firmly around his, Camille didn't let go until they'd climbed the stairs and entered her bedroom. Except for the moonlight filtering through the sheer curtains on the window, the room was dark.

"If you promise not to run off, I'll let go of your hand and switch on the lamp."

"I don't need a lamp. I have cat eyes," he said. "And you don't need to worry about me running off. Not tonight."

Not tonight. But maybe tomorrow? The question flashed through her mind, but she purposely pushed it to a dark, out-of-the-way place.

"Tonight is all that matters," she whispered. Then, rising on the tips of her toes, she pressed her lips to his.

With his arms wrapped tightly around her shoulders, he kissed her so deeply that her head began to swirl, and with the slow, drunken whirl, a kaleidoscope of colors flashed behind her closed eyelids.

When he finally lifted his head, they were both dazed and panting.

"I hope you have some sort of birth control," he said gruffly. "Because I came down here to herd cattle. Not this."

She very nearly laughed. "No worries. I take oral contraceptives. So we're good."

A long breath rushed out of him. "That's a relief. Because right now I don't think I could drive all the way to Benson for a box of condoms. And I sure as heck couldn't walk out of this room without making you mine."

Loving the sound of that, she reached for the snaps on his shirt. "And I sure as heck don't intend to let you out of this room for a long, long time."

She pulled the fabric apart and then promptly pressed a row of kisses across his chest, down the center of his abdomen, then back up to one flat nipple. He allowed her tongue to circle it once, twice, and then he was pulling her head back.

"That has to wait." His raspy voice sounded like a man in agony. "Until we get out of these clothes."

"Then let's do something about them," she said in a low, seductive voice.

Reaching up, she pushed the shirt off his shoulders and down over his wrists. As it dropped to the floor, her hands came together on his belt buckle.

"Let me," he said. "It'll go faster."

Deciding faster was better, Camille turned the job over to him and began shedding her own clothing. Once she'd stripped down to a set of lacy black lingerie, she momentarily considered leaving the last two garments on, then just as quickly decided against it. She didn't want anything, not even two strips of tiny fabric, coming between them.

Once she was finished, she looked over to see he'd sunk onto the edge of the bed to pull off his boots.

She quickly swept his hands aside. "Let me do that chore for you, cowboy."

Leaning back on the mattress, he lifted both legs, and

Camille went to work removing his boots. They slipped off easily and after setting them aside, she tugged his jeans and boxers down over his feet.

The last of his clothing had hardly had time to hit the floor before he leaned up and snaked an arm around her waist. He pulled her down beside him and Camille couldn't get her arms around him fast enough.

He turned on his side and, with a hand at the back of her waist, pressed the length of her body close to his.

"Camille," he whispered against the side of her hair. "I can't believe I have you next to me—like this."

The awe in his voice matched the same wondrous feeling rushing through her. It was euphoric to the point of being scary, she thought. Having Matthew's naked body next to hers wasn't supposed to feel this good. But it did, and she couldn't wipe the smile from her lips or stop her hands from racing over the hard muscles of his arms and back.

"And I can't believe how incredible it feels to touch you. To have you close." She thrust her hand into his hair and allowed the blond curls to slip slowly through her fingers. "I've been dreaming about this—about us. If this is a dream, Matthew, then don't let me wake up."

In the moonlight, she could see his eyes sweeping over her face, and for a moment she thought she saw something real and tender in the gray depths.

"You're not dreaming, sweetheart. Let me prove it to you."

With that, he covered her lips with his in a kiss that was so all-consuming she could only grip his shoulders and hang on for dear life. But he didn't stop with just one kiss. He planted several more of them on her eager lips before he finally departed her moist mouth and started a downward trail to her breasts.

By the time he reached one nipple, Camille's breaths were coming in short, shallow sips. Her limbs felt heavy and lifeless, while the rest of her body felt as though it had been torched by a thousand sunbursts.

He suckled the center of her breast until the needy ache inside her became so unbearable, she lifted his head from the throbbing nipple.

"Matthew—I can't keep waiting!"

"Yes—you can," he said thickly. "Just a little longer."

Before she could protest, his head dropped back to the other breast, and for long moments he gave it the same erotic treatment as he had the other. And then, seemingly satisfied that he'd branded that part of her body, his mouth moved away from her breasts and began a downward trail, along her rib cage and onto her stomach.

When he reached her belly button, he paused long enough to circle it with the tip of his tongue before he moved lower still. The pulsating ache between Camille's thighs had reached the point of agony, and she was about to push his head completely away when his tongue suddenly touched the intimate folds of her womanhood.

"Oooh, Matthew! I— this is—too good—too much!"

As she spoke the last words, his tongue slipped inside and the erotic sensation caused the last thread of her self-control to unravel. Undulating waves of pleasure rippled through her body until she was nothing more than a feather in the wind, floating, twisting helplessly back and forth until consciousness finally returned.

Through a foggy daze, she recognized her hands were clenching fists full of his hair and her legs were wrapped around his waist. She allowed both to fall away from him and he immediately moved up and positioned himself over her.

Breathing hard, she lifted her gaze to his. "If you're trying to kill me, you're coming awfully close."

Smiling, he bent his head and rubbed his cheek against hers. "I'm only trying to please you, sweet Camille. That's all."

She framed his face with both hands and lifted it just enough for her to look into his eyes. "Everything about you pleases me, Matthew."

He smiled down at her. "Even my stubbornness?"

"Even that," she said with a sigh, then pulled his mouth down to hers.

He was quick to take control, and as he kissed her, Camille tasted hot desire, but something else, too. Something very sweet and very tender and so strong it brought a rush of tears to her eyes.

Not wanting him to feel the salty moisture on her cheeks, she furiously blinked it back and slipped her arms around him.

The kiss stoked the fire that was already burning between them, and the familiar ache to her body connected to his started all over again.

To her relief, he didn't make her wait. He entered her with one smooth thrust and then they were both moving together as one, giving and taking with a need so fierce it robbed the breath from her lungs and set her mind free of every single thought but him.

After a long time, or maybe only a few short minutes—Camille couldn't know because she'd lost all sense of time—she felt Matthew urging her faster and faster to the edge of a deep abyss. She didn't want to go there. Because she knew that once she fell, the incredible pleasure he was giving her would all end.

Yet no matter how much she stubbornly tried to hold back, his kisses and the driving thrust of his hips kept tugging and pulling forward, until she had no choice but to follow him.

She heard the harsh intake of his breaths above her, and then he was repeating her name over and over as he clutched her hips and poured himself into her.

Camille clung to him tightly and as she buried her face against his damp chest, she knew her life had been forever changed.

Chapter Seven

Matthew turned his head on the mattress and looked at Camille's tangled hair and sweat-sheened face. Her eyes were closed, but not in sleep. Her breasts were still rising and falling at a rapid pace, and beneath his hand, he could feel the wild thump of her heart.

The past few minutes had stunned him, and as his gaze slipped over her smooth little nose and perfectly bowed lips, he wondered if this was how it felt to actually make love.

Matthew didn't know. He only knew that it hadn't been anything like the sex he'd had with his ex-wife, or any other woman for that matter. This union with Camille had been mind-bending, and he still wasn't sure his senses had returned to full working order.

Her hand moved gently against the middle of his chest. "Mmm. I think we should get under the covers. Don't you?"

No, he thought. He should get out of her bedroom as fast as he could. But that idea was totally ludicrous. He could no more leave her side than he could cut off his arm.

"Are you cold?" he asked.

"A little."

"Then we'll get under the covers," he told her.

They both shifted around on the bed until their heads were resting on the pillows and a comforter was covering their bodies.

She snuggled her face into the curve of his neck, and Matthew lifted a long strand of her hair and tested the silky texture between his fingers. Touching her was a precious gift, and he decided that until his time here at Red Bluff was over, he was going to take all the gifts she offered him. Because once he went back to Three Rivers, he knew this thing with her would be over.

"You smell like lily of the valley," he said as he nuzzled his nose in the side of her hair.

A wan smile touched her lips. "How do you know about lilies of the valley?"

"My mother used to wear that scent. That is, whenever she had the money to buy a small bottle."

"It's a simple, old-fashioned fragrance. I suppose that's why I like it. That, and my Great-Grandmother Hollister used to wear it. When I was a little girl she would let me brush her hair and if I did a good job, she'd treat me by dabbing lily of the valley on my neck and wrist. It made me feel like a princess."

"Does it make you feel like a princess now?"

Her fingers slid up and down his arm. "No. But it fills me with warm memories of her and that's even more special."

As he absently stroked his fingers through her hair, he thought about her family and how, in many ways, she was a frontier princess. From the day she was born, Camille's roots were already set deep and solid, whereas Matthew's were so shallow and weak it was a miracle he'd managed to grow into any kind of decent man. The differences between them were staggering, yet here in her bed, with her hands touching him so tenderly, it felt like he belonged in her life and she in his.

"Three Rivers Ranch has been around so long it's a part of Arizona history. I've often wondered what it feels like to come from that sort of legacy. God knows, I'll never experience the feeling."

Her arm settled across his chest and she hugged him close. "You've been at Three Rivers for fourteen years. You've become a part of the family."

In many ways that was true, Matthew thought. Joel and Maureen had taken him in and treated him like a son. He would always love them for giving him a home.

"In a way," he agreed. "But that doesn't change the fact that I'm a Waggoner. Ask anyone around Gila Bend what that name means. My father and uncle left their own kind of legacy."

"You're not in Gila Bend anymore," she gently reminded him. "And you're making your name into something to be proud of."

"Hmm. Right now you're feeling soft and generous. In the daylight you'll see me differently."

She pressed a tiny kiss to the side of his neck. "I've studied you close up in the daylight and I like what I see."

"That's because you're wearing rose-colored sunglasses."

Smiling, she gently pinched his arm and then she

let out a wistful sigh. "Sometimes, Matthew, being a Hollister isn't easy. Did you know the ranch has been going since 1847?"

"Yes."

"Most all of the Hollisters have devoted their lives to the ranch. Some of them even lost their lives in a range war. And then there are the ones like me and Viv, and Joe. And Uncle Gil. He left Three Rivers and became a lawman. He's the reason Joe got the itch to be a deputy."

"And where did you get the itch to be a cook? From your great-grandmother who wore lily of the valley?"

She laughed softly and he momentarily closed his eyes and enjoyed the light, tinkling sound. Until he'd gone to work for the Hollisters he'd never heard much laughter. Oh, Renee had laughed, he thought. But most of the time it had been a cynical sound directed at him. She'd rarely laughed with him. But why would she? Nothing about living with him had made her happy.

As though Camille had been reading his mind, she suddenly asked, "Why did you ever marry Renee?"

He grimaced. "Don't you think this is an awkward time to be asking me that question?"

Propping up her head with her hand, she gazed down at him. "No. I happen to think it's the perfect time. Because I've wondered if you ever wanted her back in your life. In your bed."

He moved his head back and forth against the pillow. "I married Renee because I was very young and didn't know any better. I thought we would be partners. And at that time in my life I really needed one. Someone at my side to support me and encourage me." He paused and let out a cynical snort. "Hellfire, I've never been so wrong about anyone as I was about her. She had no intentions of ever being a cowboy's wife. As soon as the ink dried on the marriage license, she tried to change me. When I refused, she lit out. It was that simple. And no, once she was gone, all I felt was relief. And stupidity."

Her blue eyes traveled softly over his face. "That's the way I felt about Graham," she admitted. "Stupid."

"So why did you ever get engaged to him? I knew right off that he was a jerk."

She let out a low, self-deprecating groan. "I thought being engaged to a rich banker's son would show everybody that I wasn't just the spoiled baby Hollister. I had the crazy idea that being married to Graham would make everyone say, 'Look at Camille. She's really made something of herself.'"

He gave her a reproachful look. "You hardly needed him to be something."

A wry smile slanted her lips. "Dear God, do you know how glad I am that he fell in love with Crystal Thompson and asked for his ring back? I want to laugh until my sides hurt—that's how glad I am."

He smiled back at her and then, as his hand began to roam over the soft curve of her naked hip, he began to chuckle. "You know, I kinda want to laugh about it, too. Now. Now that I have you here with me. Like this."

She laughed with him and then lowered her lips to his ear. "Have you forgotten that we haven't had dessert yet? Want to go down to the kitchen and have some?"

"Mmm. I had forgotten. What did you say you made?"

"Does it matter?"

"Doesn't matter at all," he murmured. "Because my dessert is right here in my arms."

She gently sank her teeth into his earlobe. "That line is so corny it's sweet."

He flipped her over onto her back and as he gazed down at her, he trailed the tips of his fingers along her smooth cheek. "You have it wrong, Camille. This is sweet."

Lowering his head to hers, he placed soft little kisses upon her lips, until one of her hands curled around the back of his neck and anchored his mouth to deepen the kiss.

Her reaction was all it took to ignite a fire low in his belly, and the need to have her all over again caused his lips to turn hungry and urgent.

It was the need for air that finally forced their lips apart, and as her gaze locked with his, her blue eyes glittered with something Matthew had never seen before. Whether it was lust or love or something in between, he couldn't guess. Nor was he going to waste this moment wondering about it. Not when she was melting in his arms.

"Oh, Matthew, I want you—so much."

Maybe for tonight, he'd be enough for her. And maybe for the next two weeks, she'd be satisfied with just having him in her bed. But the future was a different matter.

Pushing the thought out of his head, he pressed a kiss on her forehead. "And I want you, Camille—more—than—you know."

She wrapped her legs around him and as he entered her again, he wondered how he was going to go back to Three Rivers and live without her.

Two days later, Camille locked the front door of the diner and went to work helping Peggy stack chairs as they prepared to shut down for the evening. Gideon had left a half hour ago to hurry home and get ready for his grandchildren's Halloween party, while Edie, the diner's other waitress, had left the diner before him in order to drive her sick sister to see a doctor at Benson.

The day had been busy, but Camille was too happy to be feeling tired. "When are you supposed to be at Gideon's this evening?" she asked Peggy as the women continued to place chairs atop the small square tables.

"I told him I'd be there at six thirty. I have my costume with me so I'll change after I get there."

"What are you going to be, Superwoman?" Camille asked impishly.

Peggy laughed. "I couldn't pull off a bodysuit! No. I'm going as myself—a nasty witch."

"Oh, Peg, you're hardly a witch. Maybe a witch's helper," Camille teased. "But never a nasty one."

"Ha! You've never seen me when I get out of bed at five in the morning," she said, then asked, "What are you going to do for Halloween tonight? Anything special?"

Camille's thoughts went straight to Matthew. She couldn't wait to get home to see him, to have him back in her arms. It was insane how much she wanted the man.

"No, I'll be staying home. In fact, I don't even know what I'm going to cook for supper."

Peggy groaned. "Cook again? After all the cooking you've done today? Uh—no way. Fix yourself a sandwich and have a bowl of ice cream for dessert."

Camille was about to tell her that a sandwich was out of the question when footsteps sounded behind them. She glanced over her shoulder to see Norman standing just inside the swinging doors to the kitchen. What was he doing back here? He'd left for home more than two hours ago.

"Camille, let Peggy finish the chairs. I'd like to speak with you in my office."

The short, pudgy man with thinning brown hair turned and disappeared through the swinging back doors to the kitchen. Peggy cast Camille a speculative glance.

"Wonder what he wants? Lord, I hope he's not planning on cutting our wages. I'm barely making ends meet as it is."

Shaking her head, Camille plopped the chair she was holding onto the top of a table, then started out of the room. "I don't think it's anything like that. I'm hoping he's decided to hop on the idea of the blue plate special!"

Norman's office was a little cubbyhole of a room directly behind the kitchen. The space was windowless and always hot, and since she'd gone to work for the man, she'd never once seen the top of his desk. There were too many stacks of papers, coffee cups and manila folders to actually see the wood beneath.

"You wanted to talk with me, Norman?" she asked as she stepped into the cluttered space.

He gestured to the folding chair in front of his desk. "Yes, sit down, Camille."

She moved a nylon jacket and a box of table napkins from the chair, then took a seat. "We had a whale of a lunch run today," she told him. "We're going to have to put bread, steak fingers and gravy mix on the food order list."

He waved his hand in a dismissive way. "That's not what I wanted to talk to you about. In fact, you're going to have to start taking care of all the orders and shipments."

She stared blankly at him. "Me? Why? Are you taking some time off or something?"

"Permanent time off." He turned his palms up in a gesture of resignation. "I've decided I'm going to sell the diner to you. That is, if you still want it."

Camille's heart was suddenly thumping loudly in her ears. Two months had passed since she'd made an offer to Norman for the diner, and in between then and now, he'd not given her any sort of hint as to his feelings on the matter.

Incredulous, she scooted to the edge of the chair. "Are you serious?"

He nodded. "Jan and I talked it over. I don't have to tell you I was reluctant about the idea. This place has been my baby for many years and it's been good to us." His shrug was a sign of surrender. "But we both decided that time is ticking by. We want to do some of that traveling we've always talked about."

Seeing he was actually sincere about his decision, excitement bubbled inside her. "You've stunned me, Norm. Are you sure you really want to do this?"

The smile he gave her was a bit melancholy. "Yes. With the understanding that you're still willing to give what you offered. We think it's a fair price."

"Oh, yes! The price is fine with me!" She jumped up from the chair and clapped her hands with glee. "Thank you, Norm. Thank you! This is wonderful!"

Her happy reaction caused him to shake his head with dismay. "A few months from now I hope you still feel the same way. Running this place isn't easy, Camille. I don't have to tell you that it's more than just cooking. There's finding the right food distributors, keeping deliveries on schedule, the utilities and licenses and insurance. I could go on and on, you know."

"I'm not blind, Norm. I've seen how hard you work and everything it involves, but I believe I can handle the job."

"Good. I'm glad you feel confident about it. Now I can go home and give Jan the news. I promised to take her to Tucson tonight. It's our wedding anniversary and she wants to go shopping."

"Congratulations! You've sold the diner, so tell Jan she can buy as much as she wants," Camille joked.

He let out a mocking laugh. "Ha! Technically I've just become unemployed. She'll have to cut back on her spending."

Camille laughed. "Norm, you can't fool me. I'll bet you have the first penny you ever made."

He smiled knowingly. "Not exactly. But I will say the diner has been good to me. And I hope it will be just as successful with you at the helm, Camille."

"Thank you, Norm." She reached across the desk and shook his hand. "So, when do you want to officially do the deal? I'll need to make some banking arrangements."

"I'll have the papers drawn up next week," he told her. "In the meantime, you might want to give Peggy and Gideon and Edie the news. Just in case they hear a rumor and worry. Jan says she won't say a peep, but that's like me saying I won't eat a bite of your pie."

Camille laughed. "Okay. And they needn't worry. I'd never dream of replacing them. They're like family."

Norman nodded, and after they discussed a few more minor details about the sale, he ended the meeting and left for home. Once he was gone, Camille raced into the dining area, where Peggy was just finishing the mopping.

She grabbed her friend around the waist and with a loud whoop, swung her around in a joyous circle.

"Camille!" the waitress exclaimed. "What the heck are you doing? My floor! We're making tracks on my wet floor!"

Laughing, Camille tugged her into the kitchen and after pushing her down on a step chair, explained that she was buying the diner from Norman.

"You're kidding, right?" Peggy asked in disbelief.

"No. I'm very serious. The diner is going to be mine. We're doing the deal next week."

"Oh, my word! This is unbelievable. I knew that you pitched the idea to him about the blue plate special, but I had no idea that you'd tried to buy the place!" Peggy shook her head. "Uh—Camille, are you absolutely sure about this? Look at what running the diner all these years has done to Norman. He's bald and overweight and has high blood pressure."

Undaunted, Camille shook her head. "I understand it will be lots of work. But I intend to run the place a little differently, and if business picks up and we need more help, I'll hire more help. Until then, you and Gideon and Edie will be my extra helping hands. And don't worry, I intend to keep your salaries and benefits as they are. And possibly make them better."

As the reality began to sink in for Peggy, she gathered Camille in a tight hug. "This is just wonderful, Camille. Now I don't have to worry about you leaving and going back to Three Rivers."

Camille smiled wanly. "No. My home is on Red

Bluff now. And I don't expect my family is going to be thrilled with the news about the diner. But I think they'll eventually get used to the idea." The faint smile fell from her face as she suddenly thought about Matthew. Her darling Matthew. In a way, their relationship was just now beginning, but to Camille it felt as though she'd loved him for ages and ages.

Loved him? No, Camille. You don't love Matthew. At least, not yet. You love how he makes you feel. You love to look at him, listen to his voice and have his arms around you. You need to have him near and want to believe that he needs the same from you. But to love him with the deepest part of your heart? To spend all the days of your life with him? No. It's too soon for you to feel that much.

"Camille? What's wrong? You look sad. Are you worrying about your family?"

Shaking her head, she gave her friend a reassuring hug. "No. I'm not worried about them. I was just thinking—about someone and wondering how he's going to take the news."

Peggy's dark eyes narrowed with speculation and Camille blushed under the scrutiny.

"He?" she questioned. "I didn't realize you had a man in your life."

"I didn't realize it, either. Until recently." Pausing, Camille let out a sigh that was both dreamy and hopeless. "I—you see, I've known this man since I was a teenager, but we were never close—I mean, other than casual friends. And since I moved down here to Red Bluff, I'd not seen him in more than two years. Not until he and some of the ranch hands came down this past week to move cattle onto the grazing ranges."

"So he's a cowboy?"

Camille nodded, while thinking the term didn't begin to describe all the things that Matthew was as a man and as the foreman of Three Rivers Ranch.

"He's the foreman of my family's ranch and has been since around the time my father died."

Peggy's lips formed a big round O. "That was several years ago. Why are you just now developing a thing for this man?"

Camille had asked herself that very same question and she'd come to the conclusion that there was not one certain answer. "First of all, he was married a long time ago. That's when I was a senior in high school. She was a fluff head and it didn't last long. After that, he pretty much shied away from women. Which was understandable."

"Hmm. Because after her, he couldn't trust women?" Peggy asked.

Shaking her head, Camille said, "I think it was more like he couldn't trust his judgment in women."

Peggy slanted her a meaningful look. "I've heard you say the same thing about yourself and men. But if you're seeing this guy, then you've obviously gotten rid of that fear."

No, Camille thought, she was a long way from getting over that anxiety. Maybe if she knew for certain that Matthew loved her, she'd feel confident about him, about herself and the future. But since the night he'd gone to bed with her, Matthew hadn't come close to voicing the *L* word to her. In fact, he'd skirted so far around it that sometimes she felt the chasm between them was as wide as the Grand Canyon.

"I'm trying to get past that. And I believe he's trying, too," she said. Then, with a rueful groan, she sank onto the wooden stool sitting near the work counter and covered her face with her hands. "Oh, Peggy, I'm so mixed up. I'm thrilled and happy and worried all at the same time. I don't know what's going to happen with me and Matthew. He'll be going home in another week or so and I have this terrible feeling that he won't be back. Not until next fall."

Frowning, Peggy questioned, "Next fall? I don't know a whole lot about ranching, but if the cattle are here for the winter, won't he have to come back in the spring to get them and take them back to the other ranch?"

"You're right. Come spring, most of the cows and calves will be moved back to Three Rivers. But at that time of the year Matthew doesn't come down here to Red Bluff. It's a terribly busy time at the big ranch. What with spring roundup and branding, my brother, Blake, can't spare Matthew. He sends a different crew of ranch hands down here in the spring. And anyway, seeing a man, even twice a year, couldn't be counted as a relationship."

"I see about the ranching and the cattle. But I don't see everything about you. Or maybe I do," she said. Then, leaving her seat on the step chair, she walked over and placed a steadying hand on Camille's shoulder. "I'm getting the feeling, my dear friend, that you're falling for this guy in a big way."

Dropping her hands away from her face, Camille looked uncertainly at the other woman. "Okay, Peggy, I'll be honest. I'm getting the feeling that I'm falling for him, too. He makes me happier than I've ever been in my life. But he's been divorced for nearly ten years and ever since then he's chosen to remain single. He doesn't want a wife or children. That doesn't leave me with anything except a short, hot affair."

Thoughtful now, Peggy walked to the end of the cabinet and dumped the grounds from the industrial-sized coffeemaker. "Now you're buying the diner. Which means your life is going to be here, while his life is up in Yavapai County. It might be a little hard to have any kind of affair with more than two hundred miles between you."

Sighing, Camille slipped off the stool. "I can't worry about that. I tried giving up my wants and wishes for a man before and it didn't work. I'm not going to give up my dream for this diner, or my home on Red Bluff. I can't see how Matthew and I can happily fit our lives together. But I'm hoping for a miracle. They do happen, you know."

Peggy made a cynical grunt. "Maybe at Christmastime. But today is Halloween. You're a long way off from a Christmas miracle."

Chapter Eight

"You wanta go to Benson with us tonight, Matthew?" Pate asked him as he and the rest of the men unsaddled their mounts. "It's Halloween. We want to see if we can go stir up a bit of mischief."

As TooTall predicted, yesterday they'd captured the last four steers and turned them in with the other sixteen to be shipped to Three Rivers. Today Matthew, TooTall, Pate and Abel had moved two separate herds to the eastern slopes of the ranch. The area had been thick with more chaparral and Matthew knew his horse was probably carrying just as many thorns in his hide as he was in his arms. The notion of going out on the town was enough to make him curse.

"No. Not interested in going to Benson. And the mischief better not be any more than drinking a beer or two," he warned the young cowboy. "I don't aim to bail any of you out of jail."

"Aww, Matthew. Sometimes you act like an old man. Don't you ever wanta have fun?"

"Depends on what you call fun." Matthew hefted his saddle onto his shoulder and started into the tack room, all the while thinking that young Pate wasn't all wrong. In many ways, Matthew was like an old man, because he'd never had the chance to be a child or a teenager. He'd been too busy trying to work at any kind of job he could find to help his mother and sister and himself stay afloat. Fun had always been something for the other kids to have, not Matthew Waggoner.

"Don't worry, Yellow Hair," TooTall said as he followed him into the tack room. "We won't let the little greenhorn do anything silly."

Matthew said, "I'm not worried, TooTall. Just be careful driving. That's all I ask."

TooTall hung a bridle and breast collar on pegs running along one wall, then turned and glanced at Matthew. "You look tired, friend."

"I'm okay," he replied. "We had a long day."

"Yes, but a good day. You should be happy."

"I am happy, TooTall. See?" He plastered a wide grin on his face.

His eyes narrowed shrewdly, TooTall waved a dismissive hand at him. "That's phony. Not honest."

Sighing, Matthew sat down on a low wooden bench and began to unbuckle his spurs. "Okay. Whatever you say, TooTall."

"I say you have a sickness. In here."

Matthew glanced up to see the ranch hand tapping a finger to the middle of his chest. The idea that TooTall could be so damned perceptive was downright annoying and he couldn't help but glare at him.

"I don't have any kind of sickness," he retorted.

"Yes," he countered. "Are you homesick?"

Homesick. That might be the perfect word for what he was feeling, Matthew thought. He was homesick but not for Three Rivers. He was sick from continually longing for something he knew he couldn't have. Like having Camille as his wife and the mother of his children. Like having a real home with her, where they would always be together. Where she would never walk away from him for any reason.

"No. I'm tired and I'm hungry. And I'm thinking we'd better check the water well pumps in Coyote Valley before we put in cattle there."

"Coyote Valley? Are we going there tomorrow?" Abel asked as he entered the tack room carrying a stack of sweaty saddle pads. "That's miles away from the ranch yard."

"That's right," Matthew told him. "So you guys better not get sick tonight on Halloween candy. You're going to have a hard day in the saddle tomorrow."

"Halloween candy?" Pate asked blankly as he joined the group in the tack room. "Who's going to be eating candy? I thought we were going to the Trail's End."

Abel rolled his eyes. "He's talking about the liquid kind, goofy."

"Oh. Well, don't let one little worry go through your head, Matthew," Pate said smugly. "I'll make sure everybody stays in line."

Abel grabbed the young cowboy by the back of the collar and playfully kicked him out the door.

TooTall patted Matthew's shoulder. "You go on to the house, Boss. I'll take care of your horse."

"He has thorns," Matthew told him.

"I'll take care of him," he reiterated. "You go."

Matthew thanked him and left the tack room.

Outside, darkness shrouded the ranch yard and with the disappearance of the sun, cool air had moved in. After working in the heat all day, the drop in temperature put a spring in his step and he turned the long walk to the ranch house into short work.

When he stepped up to the back door, he noticed there were no lights on in the kitchen. Which was unusual. At this time of the day, Camille wouldn't be anywhere else. But to give the men a much-needed break, Matthew had called it a day a little earlier than usual this evening. She might be upstairs in the shower, or changing out of the clothes she'd worn to work.

After letting himself in, he discovered the kitchen was quiet, along with the rest of the house. The cold greeting pointed out just how much he'd come to expect being greeted by Camille's warm smile and even warmer kiss.

Well, you might as well get used to this, Matthew. This is the way it's going to be when you go home to Three Rivers. No dinners or conversation. No teasing or laughter. And especially no loving arms wrapped around you or kisses to send you to paradise. So get used to it, cowboy. You made your bed with Camille, but it's not going to last forever.

Shaking away the miserable voice going off in his head, Matthew quickly stripped out of his dirty clothes and stepped into the shower. At least he'd be clean whenever Camille did show up.

He'd dried off and pulled on a pair of jeans when he heard Camille's light footsteps scurrying down the hallway, and then she was standing in the open doorway, her face a beaming picture of sunshine.

"Knock, knock! May I come in?"

Damn, but it was crazy how just the sound of her voice thrilled him, he thought. He grinned at her. "Sure. I don't think I could stop you anyway."

She walked into the room and didn't stop until she'd smacked a kiss on his lips. "I'm sorry I wasn't here when you got home. I was detained at the diner by my boss. Or I guess I should say used-to-be boss."

He studied her sparkling blue eyes. "Maybe you should explain that part about used-to-be."

With a light laugh, she wrapped her hand around his and tugged him over to the bed. "Let's sit while I explain."

He slanted her a wry look. "You think this is safe sitting here?"

She chuckled. "I think we can control ourselves for a few minutes. So let me tell you what's happened. It's very exciting."

An uneasy feeling rippled through him. "Okay," he said. "What's happened?"

The smile on her face grew even wider. "Norman is selling the diner to me! That's why I'm late. He wanted to talk it over with me to make sure I was still interested."

"And you told him that you were?"

"I couldn't get yes out fast enough!"

Matthew could see she was on the verge of jumping up and down with glee and he wanted to share in her happiness. But her announcement was the same as erecting a fence between them. She was digging her roots here in Cochise County, far away from him. And yet, he couldn't blame her for going after what she wanted in her life.

"This is big news," he said. "So, when will you be making the deal?"

"Sometime next week, after Norman gets the paperwork together." She squeezed his hand. "Oh, Matthew, I'm so excited. There's so much I want to do with the place. Changes I want to make with the menu and the building itself. It's going to be a lot of work, but that just makes something more worthwhile, don't you think? When you invest your all in it?"

Yes, Matthew knew about investing his all into something. For the past fourteen years, he'd invested his whole life into Three Rivers Ranch. He meant something there. His work was important and so was his relationship with the Hollister family. He could never leave it.

He gave her a wan smile. "Sure it does. And I'm happy for you, Camille. I hope it's a huge success for you."

Her beaming expression turned doubtful. "Are you really happy for me, Matthew?"

He cupped his hand to the side of her face and she immediately rubbed her cheek against the callused skin of his palm. She was the most sensual woman he'd ever known and just looking at her turned him on. After making love to Camille, no other woman would do. So where did that leave him?

His throat suddenly felt like someone was choking him. "I meant what I said. Why? You don't believe me?"

She shrugged and looked sheepishly down at their clasped hands. "Yes—but I honestly wasn't expecting you to say that. I thought you'd be chastising me for jumping into something so—well, big. Under the best of circumstances, the food service business is iffy. I could possibly fail."

Her gaze lifted back to his face and the look in her

blue eyes was so tender he almost believed it was love. But what did he know about love? he cynically asked himself. He probably wouldn't know the emotion if it slapped him in the face.

"You're not going to fail, Camille. I have faith in you."

His words put the sunny smile back on her face and with a little cry of joy, she wrapped her arms around his neck. "Matthew, you can't know what that means to me. Especially when I think of what my family is going to say when they get the news. Especially Blake. He's not going like it at all."

He circled his arms around her. "Blake is living his life the way he chooses. You should have the chance to do the same."

She reared her head and looked at him. "I think you honestly mean that."

"Why wouldn't I? Renee tried to change me and made me miserable in the process. No one should try to change you, either."

She gave him another soft, melting look, then pulled out of his arms and stood. "Thank you, Matthew. Now I'd better go find something to fix for supper. It's Halloween! Or have you forgotten about it?"

Rising to his feet, he reached for the clean shirt that he'd laid on the end of the bed before his shower. "No. I've not forgotten. Tonight is for treating. I thought we might drive over to Benson and have dinner out. We've not ever been anywhere together."

She leveled a mischievous look at him. "We've been to bed together," she pointed out. "But that's not like a date, is it?"

He laughed. "Not exactly."

Laughing with him, she hurried toward the open

doorway. "Okay, give me a few minutes to get out of these greasy clothes and fix myself up."

"You got it," he told her.

She vanished from sight, and Matthew could hear her light footsteps racing down the hallway, then climbing the stairs to her bedroom. As he shrugged into his shirt, he walked over to the dresser mirror and stared at his image.

Everything looked the same, he thought. And yet, everything inside him felt different. How in hell could he be so encouraging and thoughtful at a time like this? She might as well have planted a flag out in the court-yard that read, *I'm here to stay and to hell with Matthew Waggoner.*

Muttering a curse under his breath, he reached for a hairbrush and tugged it through his damp blond curls. There wasn't any reason for him to be anything but en-couraging and thoughtful. Just because they were hav-ing a sexual relationship didn't mean she cared about him. Really cared, like I'll-follow-you-to-the-ends-of-the-earth kind of caring. So he needed to snap out of it and get real. This thing with her was just a pleasur-able escapade, a brief break from his days of horses and cattle and corralling a group of cowboys.

Camille and Matthew had dinner at a modest little Mexican café located on the edge of town, not far from the Trail's End nightclub where Pate and the guys had gone to kick up their heels.

The food was delicious, but Matthew could've been eating bread and carrot sticks and washing it down with water and he wouldn't have known the difference. He wasn't sure what exactly Camille had done to herself to-night, but she looked like a piece of treasure all wrapped in a gold-and-brown-patterned dress that clung to her curves and pulled out the fiery glints in her hair. Her hair was different, too. The long strands were looped and pinned to the top of head, while a few of them had been left loose to trail down the middle of her back. Large gold hoops swung in her ears, and red lipstick made her whole face glow.

Hell, he wasn't supposed to be with a woman like this, he thought. She was so far out of his league, it was laughable. But he wasn't laughing. His heart wasn't in the mood for it.

"They make great tres leches cake here," Camille told him. "If you're hankering for dessert."

"I'm full to the brim," he told her. "But you get a piece if you like."

She shook her head. "Actually, there's something else I'd like to do. If you're agreeable, that is."

He pushed his plate away. "What is it?"

She cast him an eager smile. "On the way back to Red Bluff, I thought we might swing by Dragoon. I'd love to show you the diner. It's closed, obviously, but I have a key."

He could see just how much it meant to her, and the fact that she wanted to share this part of her life with him made him feel just a bit special.

"I'd like that."

He motioned to the waiter and after he'd taken care of the bill, they left the café. As Matthew drove his truck east toward Dragoon, Camille put the subject of the diner aside and instead questioned him about his day.

Then she said, "You're probably going to laugh at this, but I've been thinking about getting one of the paints out and riding next Sunday after church. That's about the only day I have for it."

Surprised, he glanced at her. "How long has it been since you've ridden?"

"Oh, not that long ago. When Hannah and Nick come down, I usually try to ride once or twice with them. Of course, you have to be ready for a marathon ride with those two. They never want to get out of the saddle."

Vivian's daughter, Hannah, and Blake's son, Nick, weren't just cousins, they were the best of friends and both shared a love of horses. Occasionally Vivian would bring the two kids down so they could ride over the more gentle areas of Red Bluff.

"I can't recall the last time I saw you on a horse," he said.

She laughed. "It's not always a pretty sight, but most of the time I don't hit the dirt."

They traveled a mile or more in silence before he said, "Actually, Blake has given me another job besides moving cattle."

Camille frowned. "What's come over him? Is he becoming a taskmaster or something?"

"No. He's asked me to stay a few days longer than we'd first planned on. He wants me to look over the whole property. He's thinking about running more cattle down here year-round."

Wide-eyed, she turned slightly toward him. "Seriously?"

"That's right. Three Rivers has been thriving. He wants to invest and broaden its assets."

She shook her head. "But he needs the space down here for winter grazing. That won't work if he has it full of cattle all year long."

"Good deduction, Camille. You are truly a rancher's daughter."

"Thanks. But even a child could see the problem with running out of grazing land."

"Nothing concrete has been said to me, but I'm getting the impression that Blake and your mother are planning on purchasing more land down in this area. If they can find something suitable."

"Hmm. That's very interesting. But what has any of that got to do with me horseback riding?"

"Well, it means I'm going to put you to work. We can ride together and you can help me look the land over."

A wide smile spread over her lips and then she laughed. "Oh my goodness, the foreman of Three Rivers Ranch is going to see how I sit a saddle! Okay. But you promise you won't laugh at me?"

"I promise I'll never laugh at you, Camille. With you. But never at you."

She reached for his hand and when she lifted the knuckles of his fingers to her lips, he wanted to stop the truck on the side of the highway and pull her into his arms. He wanted to tell her all the wants and wishes and feelings that were swirling inside him and tearing at his heart.

But he couldn't expose himself like that to her. She wasn't in this thing with him for the long haul. All she wanted from him was sex.

Yeah, wouldn't it be great, Matthew thought, if he could go back to the days when sex was all *he* wanted.

Chapter Nine

The Lost Antelope was a long, squatty building with stucco walls painted turquoise. The roof was terra-cotta tiles and the window frames and door were stained dark brown. Two large plate glass windows sat on either side of the door. In the left window, a neon sign advertised a popular beer, while in the opposite window hung a metal sign that simply read: Good Food.

The parking area was plain dirt with a faint bit of gravel left over from years gone by. At the back of the building, a rickety windmill was shrouded with mesquite trees.

Camille's beloved diner was like nothing he'd been expecting, and for long minutes after he cut the truck motor, he simply stared out the windshield.

"What's wrong? You're not saying a word," she said.

"No. I'm thinking."

"Well, if you were expecting a fancy café with outdoor seating and half-naked waitresses serving espressos, then you should be disappointed. It's just a simple place with good food—just like the sign says."

"I'm not disappointed," he told her. "I'm surprised, that's all. It just doesn't seem your style."

"Hmm. What is my style, Matthew? Something more modern and expensive-looking?"

"All right, I confess," he said sheepishly. "I was thinking along those lines."

She cast him a reproachful look before she shoved off her seat belt and opened the truck door. "Come on. Let's go in and I'll show you around."

He walked at her side across the hard-packed ground to the back of the building, where a security light illuminated a single metal door.

Since the diner sat on a lonely spot near the highway and wasn't exactly a part of the tiny settlement of Dragoon, Matthew wouldn't be surprised to learn it was often vandalized—although he couldn't see any sign of prior damage to the door or the walls of the stucco structure.

"How many times has this place been robbed?" he asked.

"Never. Norman always takes the money home with him in the evening. I like to believe little desert angels guard the place, because it's never been defaced or damaged. The insurance on the property is outrageous. But that's to be expected."

She unlocked the door, pushed it open and reached around the left wall. Fluorescent lighting instantly flooded a square room with shelves built into the walls on three sides. As Matthew followed her inside, he glanced around at the industrial-sized canned goods, along with an assortment of boxes that were jammed and stacked in every available space.

"This is where we store most of the nonperishable food," she told him. "And a few odds and ends like table napkins and paper towels and that sort of thing."

He was amazed at the volume of stored food. "You actually use all this? Looks like there's enough stockpiled in here to feed a small army."

She looked amused. "Norm is ordering all the time. Otherwise, these shelves would be wiped out."

Motioning for him to follow her, she reached through an open doorway leading into a connecting room and switched on another light. As the two of them moved forward, she said, "In this area is where we keep the refrigerated and frozen foods."

Matthew glanced around at several refrigerators, the sizes ranging from small to large, plus two huge upright freezers. The floor was bare concrete and the cinderblock walls painted pale green. So far, everything he'd seen was impeccably clean and neat.

"One of the freezers is sort of iffy at times. We keep a close watch on the thermometer to make sure the compressor isn't going on the blink."

"You don't have a walk-in freezer?" he asked.

Shaking her head, she said, "No. Norm considered it, but the cost of running the thing wasn't going to be feasible."

She flipped another light switch, then pushed through a single swinging door that was colored the same green as the walls. They stepped into a small kitchen and Matthew gazed curiously around him. The space was equipped with a large flat grill and another stove with six large gas burners and an oven below. On the opposite wall from the stoves was a long row of cabinets with a wooden work counter. The scars made from cutting and chopping covered nearly every inch of the worn surface.

"And this is my domain," she said with a proud smile. "It's where I spend my days. Yours is out on the range and mine is in front of one. Only it's a different kind of range."

She was obviously in love with the place. A fact that totally mystified Matthew. She'd always been Joel's little princess and even after her father died, the rest of the family had continued to treat her as such. She'd been the pampered sibling of the Hollister clan and he couldn't ever remember seeing her with grubby hands or wearing dirty work clothes. Apparently that Camille hadn't been the person she'd wanted to be.

"Do you have everything here in the kitchen that you need? Or do you have plans for this part of the diner?" he asked.

"It's enough to get by. Later, if I see that business continues to pick up, I'd like to have a larger oven installed for more baking." She pointed to the cabinets behind him. "That's where we keep all the pots and pans and cooking utensils. Over there on the other wall are the glasses and cups and serving dishes. Although we don't use a lot of the dishes because most things are served in baskets. Which makes Gideon happy. He has less to wash."

"And Gideon is?"

"Our busboy and dishwasher. He's an older gentleman—a widower and a war veteran, in fact. He's lived in Dragoon ever since he got out of the military. Actually, he's throwing a Halloween party for his grandchildren tonight. That's the kind of big-hearted guy he is."

"Your coworker is having a party and you didn't go? Or weren't you invited?"

Her smile turned coy. "Oh, sure I was invited. But I begged off. I wasn't about to miss being with you. It's not like you'll be here much longer and I see my coworkers all the time."

Matthew felt honored that she'd chosen to be with him tonight, but it wasn't enough to overcome the sick little feeling that hit him every time he thought of their dwindling days together. "Then I'm glad we went out for dinner tonight. Your Halloween wasn't a total bust."

She wrapped her arm around his and the soft laugh that passed her lips was utterly sexy. "The night isn't over yet. And I have a few tricks and treats planned for you."

He was trying not to let his mind go there as she urged him forward and through a pair of swinging wooden doors. The security lamps out in the parking area shed plenty of light for him to see the rows of tables and chairs, plus a small checkout counter located in one corner of the room.

"Here's the dining area," she announced. "And this is where I'd like to make most of the changes. Like knocking out the east wall and adding more space. As long as a construction crew can promise to keep the outside looking exactly the same, that is. The simplicity of the place is its charm and I don't want to take that away."

She was right, Matthew thought. If she knocked this building down and replaced it with a fancy new one, she'd end up cooking for herself. "It does have character," he agreed. "What about its name? Are you considering changing it?"

She shook her head. "Not at all. There's folklore behind it. Seems as though back in the late eighteen hundreds there was a prospector camped on this spot, and one night an antelope came up to his campfire. He tried to shoo the animal away, but day after day the antelope kept returning. After a while the prospector figured out the antelope must have gotten lost from the herd and his family and friends had moved on without him."

He slanted her a droll glance. "A lost, lonely antelope, huh? Do you believe that story?"

"Absolutely. And why not? Even wild animals crave company. Like the mustangs and coyotes. They band together in families."

Yes, those wild animals had more of a loving family instinct than any of the Waggoner men had possessed, he thought ruefully. "Have you ever thought the prospector might have shot the antelope and eaten it?" he asked.

She pinched the top of his forearm. "Oh, Matthew, no! The prospector and the antelope became great buddies and lived happily ever after—together. That's how the story goes and that's why this diner will always be The Lost Antelope."

He gazed down at her and as he studied her glowing face, it struck him that her happiness meant far more to him than his own. If that meant he loved her, then he was up to his neck in trouble.

"It fits this place—and you," he said gently.

She looked up at him, and just for a second Matthew thought he saw a tremble on her lower lip. "So, what do you think about the place, Matthew? Do you believe I'm making a mistake to buy it?"

Earlier this evening at Red Bluff he probably would've told her, hell yeah, it was a whopper of a mistake. But now, seeing the diner and her in it, he'd had a complete change of heart. During the last few years she'd lived at Three Rivers, he'd never seen her looking this happy.

"It's not a mistake to follow your heart. I'm glad you've found the courage to do that, Camille. Not all of us are strong enough."

Her expression turned pensive. "You can't be talking about yourself. You're one of the bravest men I've ever known. Not for just the things you do on the job, but for all the things you've survived in your life. That takes enormous courage."

Her praise swelled his chest, yet it also made him feel like the biggest fraud ever born. Even if he'd known exactly how to describe his feelings for her, he wasn't brave enough to try to explain them to her. But then, why bother with that? he wondered cynically. His feelings wouldn't change the fact that their lives were too different to merge together on a permanent basis.

"Let's hope there aren't any Halloween goblins on Red Bluff when we get home," he joked in an effort to lighten the moment. "Then you'll see what a 'fraidy cat I am."

She chuckled. "Sure, Mr. Waggoner. Don't worry, I'll chase them away for you."

As soon as they entered the house back at Red Bluff, Camille took him by the hand, and together they climbed the stairs to her bedroom. Inside the darkened room, Camille methodically went about removing her clothes, while Matthew did the same.

It was bittersweet, she thought, how comfortable and at home they felt with each other. Like a couple who'd been together for a long, long time. Had it been only a week since he'd walked into the house and into her life? And did she only have a week plus a few more days left with him?

The questions left an aching knot in her throat, but she quickly attempted to swallow it away. Tonight was too special to ruin with worries. Like she'd told Peggy, there was always a miracle, and she was going to hold on to that hope.

Behind her, she heard a plunk and then another as his boots hit the floor. The sound was followed by the rustle of his jeans and then, just as she was unfastening the last hoop from her earlobe, he came up behind her and his strong arms wrapped around her waist.

Tossing the earring to the dresser, she turned and, with a groan of pleasure, slipped her arms around him.

"Happy Halloween, Matthew," she whispered.

He kissed her softly. "Happy Halloween to you, Camille."

Bending slightly, he picked her up in his arms and carried her to the bed. Once he was lying next to her, he rolled to his side and pulled her tight against him.

As her gaze soaked in the rugged angles and curves of his features, she traced the tip of her forefinger over his lips. "How did you celebrate Halloween when you were a child? Eat yourself sick with candy?"

He caught hold of her hand and kissed the palm. "I liked the candy, but what I remember most at Halloween was my sister telling me spooky stories. I'd be so afraid I would pull the covers over my head and cry."

"Cry?" She stroked her fingers through his hair. "Oooh, Matthew, that's—awful. Why were you so afraid? Didn't anyone explain that it was all make-believe?"

His lips twisted. "Sis would tell me later that it was all just a story and there weren't any such things as ghosts and goblins. But I didn't believe her. Why should I? All I'd ever known was bad things."

That Matthew should remember such a sad part of his childhood, a period of his life that should have been filled with joyful imagination, tore a hole right through Camille.

"Well, there're no spooky stories tonight. No bad things lurking in the shadows." She smiled gently at him. "But we can get under the covers if you like."

He smiled back at her and then, closing his eyes, he pressed his cheek against hers. "I think we'll be fine just like this."

"We'll be more than fine."

And as the two of them began to make love, Camille held onto that sweet thought.

Fridays were always extra busy at The Lost Antelope, and this Friday was no exception. It was ten thirty in the morning before Camille found the time to take a small break.

"Gideon, I'm going out back for a minute or two," she said as she passed the older man, who was up to his elbows in soapy dishwater. "If Edie takes any new orders, yell at me, okay?"

"Sure, Camille. Take your time. Maybe the lunch folks won't start for a few minutes."

Outside, at the back of the building, Camille sat down on a low wooden bench situated beneath the twisted branches of a thorny mesquite tree. The sun was already hot, but the wind was whipping around like a storm was coming, stirring up dust from the dry ground.

She pulled out her phone and, after turning her back to the wind, punched in her mother's number.

The last she'd spoken with Maureen, she and the men had finished moving the cattle from the Prescott area, but that hardly meant that her mother was sitting around sipping tea and painting her fingernails. Most likely she was down at the barns, or out riding with the boys from the bunkhouse to check on cattle.

"Hello, sweetheart," Maureen answered after five long rings. "This is a surprise to hear from you in the middle of the morning. You must've taken off work today."

"No. I finally found a minute to put up my feet. And I wanted to call and share some news with you. Are you very busy right now?"

"No. Actually, I'm here with Blake in his office. We were just discussing some things about the ranch. It's nothing urgent."

Camille let out a long breath. She'd much rather have given the news to her mother while the other woman was alone. But in the end, she supposed it hardly mattered. As soon as Camille hung up the phone, her mother would spread the news to Blake and the rest of the family anyway.

She said, "I'm glad, since I don't have much time to talk."

"Is anything wrong, Camille? You sound sort of strained."

Camille grimaced. "I'm not strained. Well, to be honest, I was dreading making this call. Because I expect you're going to be upset."

"All right. What's happened? Is Matthew okay?"

Matthew was incredible. Long before daylight, she'd woken up with his face next to hers on the pillow and they made love again before the sun had ever crested over the eastern mountains. She didn't know where the man found his energy, and frankly she was wondering where hers was coming from. It was as though being with him energized her whole body and soul.

"Matthew is fine—very busy. It's me that I'm calling about. I've made a deal with Norman—Mr. Kimball. I'm buying the diner from him. We'll be finalizing the deal in the next day or two."

A long, long stretch of silence passed before Maureen finally spoke. "I see. Well, I—honestly don't know what to say."

Disappointment fell like a heavy weight on Camille's shoulders. "Why don't you start with congratulations? That would be the nice thing to do."

Maureen said, "Your mother isn't always nice, Camille. I don't have to tell you that."

No, she thought, Maureen could be a fierce tiger when you got her riled. But Camille could be just as fierce. And determined.

"I wasn't exactly expecting well wishes from you," Camille told her. "But I did want to let you know."

"Thanks for that much," she said with plenty of sarcasm, then let out a rueful sigh. "I'm sorry, Camille. I really am. I want to be happy for you. But you know

what this means to me. I was hoping—even praying—
that you'd be coming home to Three Rivers soon. Everyone here misses you and there's no need for you to
be down at Red Bluff all by yourself. But I guess—you
coming back is out of the question now."

"Yes. My life is here now, Mom. I've been trying to
tell you and the rest of the family that for a long time.
But you've all had this crazy idea that I was down here
pining away instead of actually doing and living."

"Yes, but a diner, Camille. You're going to be sinking money into a questionable business and—"

"Mom, this diner has been a profitable business for
Norm for more than twenty years and it was a money-
maker long before he purchased the place. If I do things
right it's going to remain profitable. Or don't you think
I can manage things as well as Blake or Chandler or
Viv, or—"

"Stop it, Camille!" she interrupted. "This has nothing to do with your brothers or sister. This is about
your mother voicing her concerns about the choices
you're making!"

"I'm going on thirty years old, Mom. I have a right
to make those choices, even if you disapprove. The way
I see it, Red Bluff is an important part of Three Rivers.
I want to be here—on this end of things."

"I want to be happy for you, Camille. I honestly do.
But—"

"Then why aren't you?" Camille interrupted. "Matthew is happy for me. He thinks I'm doing the right
thing. I just wish you would believe in me as much as
he does."

There was another long pause and it struck Camille
that she'd probably said too much about Matthew. But

that was okay, too. She was tired of hiding her feelings and wants and wishes.

"Oh? You've been talking to Matthew about this?"

"Of course. He's living in the house, Mom," she reminded her. "It's not like we stare at each other in stony silence."

"Uh—no, I recall you saying how much you were enjoying his company. Well, at least you have him in your corner."

Camille very nearly laughed. "You make him sound like a traitor just because he wants me to be happy."

"No. It's not that. You just sound so different, Camille. Things are coming out of your mouth that I never expected to hear."

Camille smiled wanly. "Maybe you've just begun to really listen to me."

She sighed again. "Maybe so. But I'm beginning to wonder if I need to make a trip down there. Do I?"

"No!" she blurted, then pressed a hand to her forehead. Normally she loved for her mother to come for a visit. But she and Matthew could hardly be romantic with Maureen in the house. "I mean, yes, you're welcome if you want to come for a visit. But everything is fine here. I'm even going to get on a horse this weekend. That ought to make you happy."

"It does. But Camille, I—"

From the corner of her eye, Camille caught sight of Gideon waving at her. "Sorry, Mom. I've got to get back into the kitchen. The noon rush is about to begin." She made a kissing noise into the phone, then disconnected the call.

"I hated to interrupt you, Camille, but a whole van

of people just pulled up," Gideon told her as she met him at the door.

She grinned at him. "A whole van? That's music to my ears, Gideon."

"Matthew, what in hell is going on down there?"

Matthew pulled the phone away from his ear and stared at it like he'd just picked up a horned toad from a hot rock.

"I just happen to be working my butt off. What in hell is going on up there?" he shot back at Blake.

A stretch of silence passed and Matthew used the pause to put a few steps away from the men who were working on a dead water well pump.

"Okay. I apologize," Blake said after a moment. "I shouldn't have said that."

"No. Not in that tone of voice," Matthew agreed, then said, "But forget it. You must be having a bad day."

"A bad day? Mom just left my office in tears. They were streaming down her face like her heart is broken."

Concerned now, Matthew walked over and stood beneath the skimpy shade of a Joshua tree. "What's happened? Has Joe dug up something new about Joel's death?"

"No. Not that I know of. Dear God, as much as I'd like to have that whole issue settled, I hope nothing turns up right now. I don't think Mom could handle all of this at one time."

"All of this?"

Blake cursed under his breath. "Don't play coy, Matthew! You know what's been going on! And the fact that you're happy about it just blows my mind. Mom's, too, if you want the truth of the matter."

Matthew clutched the phone. Had the family bugged the Red Bluff house with some sort of video cameras? How else would they know about him and Camille sharing a bed every night? She certainly wouldn't have told them. Would she?

"I—uh—guess you're going to have to enlighten me, Blake," Matthew finally told him. "I'm not sure what you're talking about."

After muttering another curse word, Blake said, "That damned diner! That's what!"

"Oh." Relief rushed out of Matthew. Being Blake's right-hand man and helping him run a multimillion-dollar spread was one thing, but making love to his sister was quite another. "Well, what does that have to do with me? Camille already came to the decision that she wanted the diner long before I ever showed up down here."

"Yes, but you didn't have to encourage her, did you? She told Mom you were happy about it. Is that true?"

This was getting ridiculous, Matthew thought, and it was making him a heck of a lot more than annoyed. "You're damned right, it's true. And if you would take a bit of your time to really talk to your little sister, even come see her, then you might understand."

There was no sound on the other end of the line and then the faint shuffle of papers and the creak of a chair. Blake was clearly in his office. A place he didn't actually want to be, but being Joel's first-born had put him there, along with the man's untimely death. Maureen could search far and wide and never find a better manager of the ranch than Blake. But that wasn't where he actually wanted to be. If the truth was known, he'd rather be right here with Matthew, working on a stubborn water pump, or digging up a rotten fence post, than sitting at a desk.

"I'm sorry, Blake. I shouldn't have said any of that. It's not my place to butt into your family affairs."

"You are family, Matthew. You do have a right to say all that and more. I realize you're not down there to control Camille."

Control her? The idea was laughable. She was about as controllable as one of Holt's wild fillies. "Thank God. I'd fail pretty miserably at that job."

"Well, I'm going to try to think in positive terms about this diner thing. If you think it'll be good for her, then I have to believe it. The thing is—we were all just hoping that she'd come home."

A pain crept through his chest. "Blake, I think it's time that you and the rest of the family understand that Camille *is* home."

Chapter Ten

By the end of the next week, Matthew and the men had the cattle all settled and grazing on valley grass. The water pumps were all in good working order and the fences were sound. Their job on Red Bluff was finished.

On Saturday afternoon, as the ranch hands loaded the trucks and trailers to head home to Three Rivers, TooTall was following Matthew around like a lost pup.

"I don't like this, Yellow Hair," he said. "I want to stay here with you."

"You can't. Right now you're needed back at Three Rivers. If the weather takes a turn you men will be hauling hay from morning 'til night. I'm only going to be here at Red Bluff for few more days anyway. Just long enough to look things over."

TooTall didn't look convinced and Matthew could

tell he wanted to argue the matter. But he was a loyal hand and no matter how unhappy he was with the current setup, he wouldn't create a problem for Matthew.

As the two men walked out to where the men were loading the last of the horses, TooTall cast Matthew a determined look. "You remember what you promised," he said. "You'll let me work here with you—whenever you come to stay."

Damn it, he didn't know where TooTall was getting such an idea. It was ridiculous. Even worse, it was grating on his nerves. Trying to hold on to his patience, he said, "I haven't forgotten that I promised. But you need to get that notion out of your head, TooTall. I'll be home at Three Rivers in a few days and then you'll see that nothing is going to change. We'll be working together just like always."

Frustrated, TooTall stopped in his tracks and frowned at him. "I saw a vision, Matthew, and—"

"No, you had a dream, that's all," Matthew interrupted, not wanting to hear any more nonsense from the man. "Now get in the truck with the rest of the men before I put my boot in the seat of your pants."

To soften the order, he patted TooTall's shoulder. "I'll see you in a few days. In the meantime, I'm counting on you to keep the rest of the crew in line. Okay?"

Nodding glumly, the cowboy climbed into the back seat of the truck and shut the door. Matthew walked up to the driver's window and Pate stuck his head out.

"Drive safely, Pate. And send me a text to let me know you all got there in one piece."

"Sure thing, Matthew," he said with a toothy grin. "This couple of weeks has been a hell of a ride, huh?"

"Yeah, a hell of a ride."

He lifted a hand in farewell, then turned and walked inside the barn so he wouldn't have to watch them drive away.

The next morning, Camille was thrilled to have Matthew join her in Sunday services at the little church in Dragoon. As they sat close together on the worn wooden pew, she couldn't help but notice how closely he followed the pastor's sermon and how he knew exactly where to find certain passages in the Bible. From the time he'd become an employee of Three Rivers Ranch, she recalled that he'd attended church with the entire Hollister family. Even so, Camille had never thought of him as a spiritual man. Maybe that was because his rugged exterior had always covered up the softer, gentler parts of him.

After the service she introduced him to Peggy and Gideon, who eyed him with great interest.

"Camille tells us you've been the foreman for her family's ranch for a long time," Gideon said as the four of them stood outside the little white church. "That must be a huge job."

Matthew humbly shook his head. "Not really. I have plenty of ranch hands to help get everything done that needs to be done."

"He's being modest, Gideon," Camille told the older man. "He works long hours and deals with a lot more than punching cows. Blake couldn't run the place without him."

Peggy's all too curious gaze slipped back and forth between Matthew and Camille. "I hope you'll find time to come eat at the diner before you head back to Three Rivers, Matthew," she told him. "You need to try out some of the good things Camille cooks for the customers."

Camille didn't miss the bit of color creeping up his neck.

"I—er—I've tasted a few things that Camille has cooked," he admitted. "But if I get a chance I'll drop by the diner."

"I guess she's told you about buying the place," Gideon said to him. "We're just tickled pink about it, too. Norm is a nice boss, but he's burnt out—he needs a rest."

Peggy let out a good-natured groan. "Gideon, Norm is probably ten years younger than you!"

He laughed and winked at Matthew. "True, but he's not in as good as shape as I am. Anyway, Camille will get the old place hopping. You can bet on that."

"Yeah, we're already planning on a big Christmas around here," Peggy told him. "It would be nice if you could come down and celebrate with us. Do you get a break for the holiday?"

Matthew cast a doubtful glance at Camille and she wondered if he was thinking it was about time for her to celebrate Christmas at Three Rivers. For his sake? No. He wouldn't ask her to do anything like that. Not for him. But he might ask her to do it for the rest of her family. Even so, she couldn't. Not when she was just now taking over the diner.

He said, "Ranchers don't really get time off. This break today is about the most I ever get."

"Oh, that's too bad," Peggy grumbled. "It would be nice for Camille if you could. She gets lonely out there on the ranch, you know."

"Peggy! This isn't the time or place to be talking

about Camille's social habits!" Gideon scolded her, then clamped a hand around her upper arm. "Come on, I'm going to take the kids over to Benson for lunch. You can come along—if you think you can talk nice."

Peggy pulled a face at him. "Talk nice! Gideon, you need a good dose of castor oil and—"

Before the woman could finish, Gideon yanked her away, while giving Camille and Matthew a backward wave.

"Do they always fuss like that?" Matthew asked as they watched the pair walk to Gideon's car.

"Always," Camille said with a fond smile. "They're worse than some old married couple. Except that they're not really a couple in that sense of the word. There's a forty-year age gap between them."

With a hand against the small of her back, he urged her toward his truck. "Hmm. What's a few years? Just look at Sam and Gabby," he said.

Camille laughed. "Why, Matthew, I think you're getting a romantic streak in you."

The faint smile he gave her was more like the wave of a white flag. "You're rubbing off on me, Camille."

Two hours later, Matthew decided this had to be the best day of his life. The sky was vivid blue, the sun was warm and Camille was riding beside him. And from the happy look on her face, she wasn't the least bit worried about her riding skills. In fact, he was surprised at how confidently she handled the paint mare, Daisy.

"I don't think I've ever been this far south on the ranch before," she said as the two of them reined their horses down a shallow wash thickly dotted with sagebrush. "It's very pretty, isn't it? I'll bet if we rode to that next ridge we could see all the way to Tombstone."

"Maybe. I've never been that far, either. But there is a place you might like to see before we get to the ridge. Unless you're too tired to keep going."

"Oh, I'm not the least bit tired. This is lovely, Matthew. And it's so beautiful here."

He had to agree it was a scenic area with the sage and barrel cacti and tall saguaros covering the hills and canyons. "There isn't much grazing for cattle to be had here, but more than you'd think."

Her smile was impish. "I forget this is actually a working ride for you," she said. "So, what are you thinking so far? Think Blake is being foolish to consider putting more cattle on Red Bluff?"

"No. Not from what I've seen so far. And this area basically gets as much moisture during the year as Yavapai County, while the temperature stays warmer, so that's a plus."

They rode up out of the wash and Matthew reined Dahlia, the paint sister to Daisy, in a westerly direction. Camille guided her mount alongside his.

"I think you've been doing some major fibbing to me, Camille. You're riding Daisy like an old ranch hand. I thought you said you rarely ride."

"Thank you for the compliment," she said. "But it's true that I rarely ride."

"You know what I think? You sit the saddle like your father did."

She studied him for long moments. "That's one of the nicest things you've ever said to me."

"Well, I meant it or I wouldn't have said it."

"Yes, I'm learning that much about you," she said.

They rode along in companionable silence for a short distance and then she asked, "Matthew, do you think Major Bob caused Daddy's death?"

Her question caught him off guard and caused a frown to crease his forehead. "Your father's horse would've never intentionally harmed him. Not for any reason. You believe that, don't you?"

Her nod was solemn. "Yes. I believe it. I just wondered what you really thought. I know Mom says you and the hands are still using Major Bob on the ranch."

"That's right. Maureen even rides him on some days."

"I'm glad. Because I have a feeling Major Bob misses Daddy as much as the rest of us do."

He reached over and picked up her hand that was resting against her thigh. Then, squeezing it gently, he said, "I think your feeling is right."

She glanced thoughtfully at him. "Do you believe my brothers will ever find out what really happened to Daddy that day?"

His throat tight, Matthew shrugged. "That's tough to say. I do know that Joe is like a bulldog. Once his jaw is set, he's not going to let go until he's satisfied."

She sighed. "I've not mentioned this before, but about a month ago, Blake told me and Viv about the woman down in Phoenix. I'm sure you know what I'm talking about."

He nodded. "I know. I just wasn't sure if any of your brothers had mentioned it to you. I didn't bring it up because—well, that's your private family business."

"You are family, Matthew," she said. "So tell me, do you think Daddy was cheating on Mom?"

"Hell, no! He adored your mother."

"Strange how you can be so certain," she mused aloud. "When my own brothers have their doubts about our father."

He squeezed her soft little fingers. "It's like I told you before. It's easier to see something when you're on the outside looking in."

She smiled at him and the dark cloud that had momentarily settled over Matthew lifted.

"That's all I want to say about that," she said. "So tell me where we're going."

"We're going to ride around this next hill and then you're going to see how Red Bluff got its name."

Ten minutes later, they rode along a narrow ledge that skirted the hill. Then suddenly the rough trail dropped into a deep valley and there, straight in front of them, a cliff made of slabbed red rock towered into the sky to create a boxed canyon.

Camille automatically reined her horse to a stop and stared in awe at the incredible sight. "Oh my, this is fantastic! How did you know about this?"

"I came here a long time ago with Joel. He said it was a spiritual place. I wanted to bring TooTall here to let him see it, but we didn't have the time. He's a mystical kind of guy. I figure if he ever does see it, he'll tell me he's seeing ghost riders in the sky or something."

"Well, it does strike the imagination," she said. "Let's ride closer and dismount, shall we?"

"Sure. Follow me. From here on the trail gets narrower."

Five more minutes and they were at the base of the bluff. Camille was delighted to see a pool of water beneath a trickling spring. Nearby pines seemed to be growing straight out of the rocks.

They dismounted and tied the two horses to a desert willow growing near the edge of the water. Butterflies flittered around its purplish blooms, while high above the bluff, a hawk tilted its wings in the desert wind.

Camille sat down in the cool shade and patted a spot on the rock next to her. "Come sit next to me."

He sank down beside her, then pushed the brim of his hat back on his forehead. "This is nice."

"I could stay here forever," she said with a wistful sigh, then added with a chuckle, "Until I got hungry."

"I just wonder if this is the way it looked years ago— back before gold was discovered."

"Hmm. Probably something like this," she said thoughtfully. "Did you ever think that maybe Billy the Kid roamed through this land?"

"No. His stomping ground was New Mexico. But Wyatt Earp might've. We're not far from Tombstone. Before then, some of the Spanish expeditions could've traveled through here."

She glanced curiously at him. "You know about history?"

"A little."

"I noticed today at church that you're very familiar with the Bible."

"Yes, my mother often read passages to me and my sister. When things were really tough that seemed to bring her more solace than anything."

She reached over and laid her hand on his forearm, but there was nothing she could really say to wipe away his sad memories. All she could do was to let him know that whatever hurt him, hurt her, too.

"I hear your phone dinging," he said after a moment.

"A message," she said. "I really don't want to bother with it now. But maybe I should—just to make sure it's not an emergency."

She pulled the phone from her shirt pocket and punched open the new message. "Oh, it's from Viv. She says congratulations on buying the diner. Gosh, I do love my sister."

Camille started to put the phone back into her pocket when it dinged again and she looked to see Vivian had sent a pair of photos. One was of her and Sawyer's twin boys, Jacob and Johnny. The toddlers were both dressed like pumpkins for Halloween. The second pic caused her to gasp out loud.

"Oh, oh, Matthew, look! Roslyn and Chandler's baby was born this morning! It's a boy! Look at that precious little face!" She moved the phone over so that he could see the screen with her. "That's Chandler's hands holding him. I can tell."

"Hmm. He's bald and his eyes are squinted, but if you say he looks precious, then he does," Matthew said. "I wonder what they've named him."

"William Chandler. But Viv says Chandler is already calling him Billy."

"Chandler never was big on formalities."

Camille laughed and then suddenly, before she could do anything to stop it, the joyful sound turned to a broken sob.

Hearing it, Matthew wrapped an arm around her shoulders. "Camille, what's wrong? I thought you were happy about the baby."

Blinking back her tears, she returned the phone to her shirt pocket. "I am. I'm thrilled for my brother and for the whole family. It's just that—" She looked at him and did her best to smile. "It's like you when you talk about standing on the outside looking in. That's what I'm doing, Matthew. I see my siblings with spouses and children and I don't have that. I'm not sure I'll ever have it."

"Camille, you're still very young. Your life is just beginning."

Now was the time, she thought, if he was ever going to say that he loved her, that he wanted a life with her and the children they'd hopefully have together. But nothing like that was going to come out of his mouth, she thought sadly, and she was beginning to realize it never would.

You can't be angry about that, Camille. You can't even be sad. You knew all along that Matthew was in your life on a very temporary basis. But you wanted him. Now you want to believe in miracles. But they don't happen. Not for you.

Sighing, she nodded and forced another smile to her face. "Yes. You're right. I don't have any reason to be sad. I'm young and my dream of owning the diner has just come true. I couldn't possibly hope for more."

They remained at the bluff a few more minutes and allowed the horses to drink and doze in the shade. By then, Matthew determined there wasn't enough time before dark to make it to the last ridge marking Red Bluff's most southern boundary, so they headed back to the ranch.

For most of the ride, Camille was quiet and pensive. Matthew didn't push her to talk. He understood that the news about Chandler's baby had turned her mood melancholy and there wasn't much he could say to lift her spirits. She wanted and needed things in her life that he couldn't give her.

"I'll take care of the mares, Camille. You go on to the house," he told her as they led Daisy and Dahlia into the barn.

She frowned at him. "No. That's not the way this works. I'm going to help you," she insisted. "We're in this together."

In this together. Yes, for now, he thought. For tonight and tomorrow. That was all he could let himself think about.

"Okay," he said. "If that's the way you want it."

"I do."

She led the mare over to a hitching post and looped the reins loosely around the worn wood. Matthew followed, and side by side they unsaddled the horses and put everything away in the tack room.

After they'd finished pouring out feed and spreading hay, they walked to the house, where Camille immediately excused herself and went upstairs for a shower.

While she was gone, Matthew searched around in the refrigerator for whatever leftovers he could find and went to work heating everything and setting the table.

He was pouring tea into iced glasses when he heard her footsteps enter the kitchen, and he glanced over his shoulder to see her standing a short distance away, staring in surprise.

"What is this? You've fixed us something to eat?"

"No, you did. I only heated it up. We're having spaghetti again."

She joined him at the table. "You made salad and skillet toast," she observed.

She seemed genuinely amazed, and he grinned at her. "I can be handy whenever I put my mind to it."

"Well, I'm glad you put your mind to it. But you didn't have to do all this."

He pulled out her chair. "We're in this together. Remember?"

Her eyes were watery as she lifted her gaze to his face and for one second Matthew considered drawing her into his arms, holding her tight and letting all the things he was feeling pour out in whatever words he could find. But that wouldn't do anything, he decided, except complicate things even more than they already were.

She leaned close enough to place a kiss on his cheek. "Yes, I remember," she murmured.

Clearing his throat, he helped her into the chair, and as they began to eat, Matthew was relieved to see she was collecting her ragged emotions. Still, through the remainder of the meal, he carefully avoided mentioning her family. Instead, he urged her to talk about the diner and the friends she worked with. Gradually, she began to smile again, and so did he on the outside. On the inside, he wondered how much longer he could deal with this chronic pain in his chest and the dreadful sense he was never going to recover from this trip to Red Bluff.

Once their plates were empty, Camille rose and began to gather the dirty dishes. "I think there are brownies left. I'll make coffee to go with them."

"That would be good. I'll clear the rest of this from the table."

He'd barely gotten the words from his mouth when his phone rang. As expected, the caller was Blake and he had no choice but to answer.

"Sorry, Camille. It's Blake. I'll have the coffee later."

He carried the phone into the living room and took a comfortable seat in one of the armchairs. For the next fifteen minutes he listened to everything Blake had planned for the next month. The ranch manager's agenda didn't include Matthew spending more than a few more days here at Red Bluff.

"I don't suppose you've had much time to look at some of the remote areas yet," he stated rather than asked. "This is the first day you've had without you and the guys pushing cattle."

Matthew leaned his head back against the couch and rubbed a hand over his eyes. "Camille and I took a long ride today on one of the southern sections. The grass looked good there. We didn't have time to go all the way to the boundary fence, though. I'm thinking the eastern range should be somewhat better. It's not as hilly."

"That's the way I remember it, too," Blake said.

He didn't add anything to that and Matthew waited, expecting him to continue with the subject of the grazing land. Instead, silence stretched between them.

"Blake, are you still there?" Matthew finally asked.

"Uh—yeah. Sorry, Matthew, my mind is pretty jammed right now. Too much has been going on around here. Did I hear you right? That Camille rode with you?"

"She did. You sound surprised."

"Hell, I'm not surprised. I'm flabbergasted. What have you done to my little sister? Put some kind of spell on her?"

Matthew dropped his hand away from his eyes and stared around the shadowy room. Everywhere he looked he saw Camille's lovely face smiling at him, her eyes twinkling like the desert stars. Would it be like this, he wondered, when he got back to Three Rivers? If so, he didn't know how he'd live with it.

"No. I've not put a spell on her," he said crossly. "I've just tried to encourage her. It's not that she never wanted to be a part of the ranch, Blake. She just lacked self-confidence. Your mother and all of you siblings are a pretty hard group for her to measure up to."

Blake blew out a heavy breath. "We never expected Camille to be a ranch hand. We just want her to be a part of the family."

"She is a part of the family. In her own way—the best way for her."

Blake snorted. "If you ask me, she's still hiding and unable to face her failure."

Matthew felt like reminding Blake how he'd faced his own failure when Lenore had jilted him several years ago. For a long, long time, he'd buried himself on Three Rivers and sworn off women completely. But cutting into the man wouldn't help matters. It would only cause resentment.

"Think about this, Blake. Her brothers and sisters all have things that she doesn't have. That makes her feel lost and alone. That's why—I hope that all of you will be happy for her about the diner. That's the only thing of her own that she truly has. And she's proud of it."

Blake didn't immediately reply and after the silence continued to stretch, Matthew expected him to come back with some sort of scathing retort. But he didn't. Instead, he sounded very thoughtful and almost apologetic.

"I guess I never stopped to think about my little sister in that way. And just because I'm running the ranch doesn't mean that gives me the right to rule over the whole family. Sometimes, Matthew, I wish—"

"That Joel was still alive. And you weren't having to do some of the things you're doing now," he finished tactfully.

"Yeah," Blake said gently. "The longer I do this, the more I realize that Dad was a superman. He saw everyone as they really were and always dealt with them in the right way. Every problem that came along, he handled like a man. I can't live up to him, Matthew. It's impossible."

"You shouldn't be trying. You're Blake Hollister. Not Joel or anyone else."

"No, I'm just me," he said in a pensive voice, then cleared his throat and asked, "Did you get the news about Chandler and Roslyn's baby?"

"Yes, Viv texted Camille and sent her a photo. I'm sure they're over the moon."

"We all are. I had a hell of a time tearing Kat away from the hospital. Seeing baby Billy has sparked her maternal instincts. Before the night is over I'm expecting to hear an argument for another baby."

"Another baby? But the twins aren't that old yet!" Matthew exclaimed.

Blake chuckled. "What can I say? She loves me and she loves children. How could I possibly deny her?"

"I—uh—see your problem."

Blake let out another laugh. "Problem? Hell, Matthew, I only wish you had this kind of problem."

The two men talked for a couple more minutes before Blake ended the call. Matthew slipped the phone into his pocket and walked back out to the kitchen. The room was dark and quiet and he decided Camille must have given up on him and dismissed the plan to have coffee and brownies.

He climbed the stairs and found her in the bedroom, sitting on a vanity stool in front of the dresser mirror. She was pulling a hairbrush through her long hair, and after watching her for one brief moment, he walked up behind her and placed his hands on her shoulders.

"Let me do that for you," he offered.

Smiling faintly, she handed him the brush and Matthew began to stroke the silky strands from the crown of her head all the way down to her waist. It crackled beneath his hands as though it had a life of its own and he thought how the fiery shades of copper and ginger mixed amidst the browns fit her temperament.

"Mmm. That feels good," she said.

"My horse tells me the same thing," he teased.

She made a playful face at his image in the mirror. "I'll bet he does," she said. Then her expression turned sober. "So, what was Blake's call about? Is he needing you back at Three Rivers?"

"Not yet. He told me to stay until the end of the week. If he needs me before then, he'll let me know. In the meantime, he's sending down a skeleton crew next Monday. They'll be tending the cattle for the duration of the winter."

Her face brightened. "Until the end of the week? Really?"

He nodded, while thinking how closely his happiness was now tied to hers. As long as she was smiling he was smiling, too.

"Yes. Really."

She plucked the hairbrush from his hand and tossed it on the dresser, then rose and slipped her arms around his waist. "Then we need to make every minute count, don't you think?"

"I thought you were feeling too sad to want me in your bed tonight," he murmured.

She brought her lips within a fraction of his. "Sad? I could never be sad as long as you're here with me."

As soon as the last word died away, her lips were moving over his. Matthew closed his eyes and gladly let her kiss blot every doubt and worry from his mind.

Chapter Eleven

The next day Camille came down with the sniffles, but she didn't let it stop her from going full throttle. By Wednesday Norman had everything ready to finalize the sale of the diner and the two of them drove the twenty-minute drive over to Benson to sign the papers in front of witnesses at the title company.

In spite of constantly wiping her nose with a tissue, she was in high spirits when she arrived home that evening and she couldn't wait to show Matthew the legal paper showing she was the new rightful owner of The Lost Antelope.

When she didn't find him in the house, she immediately walked down to the barn and found him in the feed room sitting on a bale of alfalfa with his cell phone jammed to his ear.

As she entered the dusty room stacked with bags

of feed and bales of hay, he acknowledged her with a glance but continued with the conversation. Which told her the call held some importance.

Deciding to wait, she walked some distance away from him and took a seat on a ledge of feed sacks.

"Yes," he spoke into the phone. "I'd like that, too. But if you need me—yeah, I understand. It can't be helped. I'll be there in the morning—as early as possible."

He hung up the phone, and the look he directed at Camille was dark and hopeless. "That was your mother. Blake has come down with the flu and the doctor has ordered him to bed. I have to leave for Three Rivers in the morning. Somehow I'm going to have to try and fill in for him until he can get on his feet."

Camille felt as though the roof of the barn had just collapsed on top of her. "But what about Mom? She can fill in for Blake!"

He shook his head as he slipped the phone back into his shirt pocket. "Cattle buyers are coming tomorrow afternoon. But Maureen and Chandler have to go to the Prescott range. Something about a sick bull they'd had to leave behind. So that means Chandler is going to have to take time off from the clinic. And it also means that I'm going to have to leave early in the morning."

"Oh." It was the only word she could manage to say.

With stiff, jerky movements, she rose and walked toward him. "But Matthew, I was planning on you staying until Saturday morning!"

He shook his head. "I was planning on it, too. But this has put a kink in things. I'm foreman of Three Rivers, Camille. I'm needed there. To do my job and part of Blake's."

"Yes," she said dully. "It's your job. I understand."

"Do you?"

Camille did understand all too well. In simple words, Matthew's life was at Three Rivers. Hers was here at Red Bluff and never the twain would meet again. Not as they had these past couple of weeks. The short period of time had changed everything for her. She'd fallen totally and irrevocably in love and no amount of time or distance was going to change that.

"I do." Tears suddenly blurred her vision and she quickly turned and started out of the feed room. "I—I'm going to the house."

Jumping from the hay bale, he caught her by the shoulder. "Camille, you came out here to the barn for some reason. What was it?"

She dabbed her watery eyes with the tissue she'd been carrying. "Nothing important. I just wanted to show you this."

She pulled the folded document from a pocket on her jacket and handed it to him.

As he unfolded the paper and scanned the contents, she watched a myriad of feelings parade across his face. He seemed pleased and regretful all at the same time.

"I'm thrilled for you, Camille."

Was he? She wouldn't describe the look on his face as thrilled, but then Matthew had never been a man to wear his feelings on his sleeve.

What feelings, Camille? The man likes your company. He enjoys the meals you cook and the sex even more. But that's all the feelings he has for you. Don't expect to read them on his face or anywhere else. In the morning you need to tell the man goodbye, then forget him.

Wanting to scream at the hateful voice going off

in her head, she took the property title from him and stuffed it back into the jacket pocket.

"Thank you," she said stiffly. "That means a lot to me."

She started to pull away from him, but his fingers tightened on her shoulder, preventing her from taking a step.

"Camille," he said softly. "Don't you think we need to talk about this?"

Her heart pounding sickly in her chest, she forced her gaze to meet his. "About this? What is there to talk about?"

His gray eyes were suddenly full of shadows. "I don't know. I thought—" He continued to look at her while a hopeless expression crept over his face. "Well, I guess you're right. There isn't anything for us to talk about. I'd just like to ask if you think you might be coming up to Three Rivers anytime soon."

He might as well have picked up the pitchfork behind him and rammed it straight into her chest. She was hurting so badly she thought her breathing was going to stop, literally.

"No. Not now. Maybe in a few months—if all goes well with the diner," she said, her voice little more than a hoarse whisper.

A muscle in his cheek flinched, but otherwise, his expression didn't change.

"I thought you would say that."

Hoping he couldn't see the pain she was feeling in her eyes, she asked, "What about you, Matthew? Will you be coming back to Red Bluff before next fall?"

"That's a whole year from now. I can't say if I might be here before that time."

She let out a long, shaky breath and did her best to smile at him. "Well, it's been special, hasn't it? And we still have tonight."

"Yeah," he said. "We still have tonight."

Long before daylight the next morning, Camille was still sound asleep when Matthew slipped out of her warm arms, dressed quietly so as not to wake her, then walked out of the house and drove away from the ranch.

The rough dirt road carrying him away from Red Bluff was narrow and often filled with wildlife. Matthew didn't allow himself to think about anything except driving the truck safely through the cold dark morning. For several miles, Hollister land remained on both sides of him, until finally, just before he reached I-10, he passed under a formal entrance and the ranch was in his rearview mirror.

When he finally merged onto the interstate, he tromped on the accelerator and focused on one single objective. Get to Three Rivers as fast as he could and back to being the Matthew Waggoner he'd been before Camille opened the door and welcomed him inside the Red Bluff hacienda.

At the speed he was driving, he reached Benson in record time, and as the lights of the town twinkled off to his left, he was glad the highway looped around it. He didn't want to see the little café where he and Camille had gone for dinner on Halloween night. No. The sooner he forgot, the quicker he could rid himself of the hollow feeling that had settled in his chest.

Yet by the time the sun started peeping over the mountains behind him and Phoenix appeared on the horizon, the pain in his heart was unbearable and the only thing he could think about was all that he'd left behind him.

So what are you going to do, Matthew? Be like that little boy back in Gila Bend and cover your head up and cry? You knew going to bed with Camille Hollister was going to be a mistake, but you couldn't resist her. You couldn't find enough common sense to walk away from the woman. No, you had to go and fall in love with her.

Determined to drown out the mocking voice in his head, Matthew punched on the radio and turned up the volume.

Damn it, he hadn't fallen in love with Camille. A man like him didn't have the ability to give that much of himself to anyone. Not when the only two things he'd ever really known in his life were hard work and surviving. And he would survive this, he mentally contended. He had no other choice.

An hour and a half later, he drove into the Three Rivers ranch yard and parked his truck near the cattle barn where Blake's office was located. The morning was still early and as he climbed down from the cab, he noticed the ranch hands were still tending to barn chores. A few yards away from the building, Chandler's diesel truck and trailer rig was idling and ready to go.

Maureen must have been watching from the window and had seen Matthew's arrival. He didn't have time to reach the office door before she burst out of the building and ran straight to him.

Hugging him tight, she said, "Matthew, you can't know how happy I am to see you!"

Maureen had always treated him as a son and considering that he'd been here on Three Rivers since he was nineteen years old, she was more like a mother to him than an employer.

He patted her shoulder, then eased her back far enough to look her in the face. "It's good to see you, too, Maureen. But I haven't been gone that long."

"It seems like ages to me," she contradicted. "And without you here to hold things together, the men act like scattered chickens."

Maureen always did give him more credit than what was due. But what would she think if she knew he'd been spending his nights in Camille's bed? Hate him? Fire him? Yes, the woman treated him like a son, Matthew thought, but Camille was her and Joel's baby.

It was too late to be thinking about that, Matthew chided himself. Besides, everything with Camille was over. He wouldn't see her again until next fall. And by then she'd probably have a man in her life. One who would be more than willing to put a ring on her finger and give her as many babies as she wanted.

Trying to shake away those dismal thoughts, he asked, "How's Blake?"

"Confined to his bed. We're trying to keep everyone, especially the kids, away from him as much as possible. Thankfully this morning he appears to be a bit better. At least, he managed to get some juice down and a piece of toast." She shook her head. "I'm sorry you had to cut the stay at Red Bluff short. Especially when we needed you to take a closer survey of the grazing situation."

"Well, when the skeleton crew gets down there they can give Blake a report."

"Ha! Do you honestly think he's going to trust their judgment? You're his eyes and ears, Matthew. You always will be."

He didn't have the opportunity to make any kind of reply to that as Chandler walked up to join them.

"Welcome home, partner," the other man said, thrusting his hand out to Matthew as though they'd not seen each other in two months rather than a little more than two weeks.

"Thanks, Doc. It's good to be home." Normally those words would have come straight from his heart, but this morning, he wasn't even sure his heart was beating. Nothing felt the same. "Congratulations on the new baby boy. You and Roslyn must be thrilled."

Chandler's grin was ear to ear. "Oh, we kinda like the little guy. Even if he does keep us up at night."

Even in his weary state of mind, it was easy for Matthew to see that Chandler was walking on a cloud over his new son. And why not? He had an adoring wife, two beautiful children and a job he loved. The man had everything that meant the most in life and suddenly Camille's words whispered through his head.

I see my siblings with spouses and children and I don't have that. I'm not sure I'll ever have it.

Funny how clearly he could now understand why she didn't want to live here. No matter how much she loved her family, the constant reminder would be too much for her to deal with. It was almost too much for Matthew to handle.

"I'll go by the house and see the baby when I get a chance," Matthew told him.

Maureen reached over and patted his cheek. "That'll be tonight, Matthew. I'm telling Reeva to set an extra plate for you at the dinner table. I want to hear all about Red Bluff and Camille."

Oh God, how was he going to endure this?

Maureen must have caught the uncomfortable look on his face because she suddenly leaned closer and studied him through squinted eyes. "Now that I'm seeing you up close, you look piqued. Are you coming down with the flu, too?"

The Hollister matriarch was right. He was coming down with something, all right. But it wasn't the influenza. There was something broken inside of him and he had the uneasy feeling it was his heart.

"Mom, Matthew has just driven more than two hundred and sixty miles. He's tired. Quit pestering him. You and I need to get on the road and see if we can get that bull home before it comes a blizzard up there."

Matthew frowned. "Blizzard? What are you talking about? It rarely snows up that way."

"Right. But the weatherman is predicting a chance of heavy snow. And we don't want to leave old blue boy up there with a bunged up leg and no shelter," Maureen told him, then motioned to the building behind them. "Go on in the office. Flo's already at work. She'll tell you all about the cattle buyers."

Taking his mother by the arm, Chandler led her off to the waiting truck, and Matthew walked into the office building.

At the end of the room, his secretary, Flo, a red-headed divorcée in her sixties, was sitting at a large desk. She looked up. Then, seeing it was Matthew who had entered her domain, she left her chair and walked over to greet him.

Not only did she give him a hug, she gave him a kiss on the cheek. Something he'd never seen her do with anyone else.

He did his best to give her a smile. "This is some kind of welcome. What did I do to deserve this?"

"You're the only man around here with enough cow sense to fill Blake's boots. Besides that," she added cheekily, "I've missed you."

"I've missed you, too, Flo."

She laughed at that, then pinched his arm for good measure. "Come on over here and sit down at my desk. You can have some coffee and pastries while I give you all the information about the cattle buyers. They should be showing up in the next hour or so."

After filling a cup with coffee and a paper plate with a bismarck and a chocolate-covered donut, she carried the lot over to where he'd taken a seat. He wasn't hungry, but the coffee was welcomed.

Matthew thanked her, then asked, "Have these men purchased cattle from Blake before?"

"No. They're two brothers from somewhere around Modesto, California, so they've traveled a far distance to buy Three Rivers' cattle. And from what Blake says, they have plenty of money to back it up. So do your best not to blow this sale, Matthew."

She returned to her seat behind the desk and he shot her a dry look. "Well, thanks Flo, for taking off all the pressure."

"You can handle it," she said, then frowned as she ran a speculative glance over his face. "By the way, you look like hell. What have you been doing down there at Red Bluff?"

Making a big mistake? The taunting question instantly rolled through Matthew's head, but he quickly dismissed it. No matter what happened in the future, getting close to Camille wasn't a mistake. He had a mind full of precious memories now. That was more than he had before.

"The same thing I do up here," he told her.

She pursed her lips with disapproval. "Then you're doing too much of it."

She pulled a manila folder from a drawer and handed it across the desktop. "Here's most of the specifics of the pending sale. If you run into any trouble, I can get Blake on the phone. But I'd rather not unless it's an emergency."

"Don't worry, Flo. There won't be any trouble."

"Camille, this order for table nine was supposed to have fried eggs, not scrambled," Peggy told her as she carried the plate of breakfast food back into the kitchen. "Did I not write the order down right?"

Turning away from the grill, Camille searched rapidly through the stack of orders until she found the correct one. "You wrote it down right, Peg. I'm the one who messed up. For the second time this morning. I'm sorry. You probably won't get a tip out of this one, either."

"I'm not worried about a tip," Peggy assured her. "I'm more concerned about you."

Camille shook her head as she cracked three eggs onto the grill. "Don't be. I'm just having a little trouble staying focused today, that's all."

"Well, I know you've come down with a cold, but you seem really off today. Has something happened at the ranch? Or with your family?"

On the opposite side of the grill, she flipped three pancakes. "The only thing that's happened is something good. Chandler and Roslyn have their new baby now. It was a boy. William Chandler Hollister. Seven pounds and four ounces and very little hair. When we get an extra minute, I'll show you a picture on my phone."

"Oh, that's exciting. You have a new little nephew! So why is your face so glum?"

Glum? She wasn't just glum, Camille thought. She was dead. At least, dead on the inside.

Matthew was gone.

This morning at five she'd woken to find her bed empty and a simple little note left on the kitchen table.

It's been nice. Matthew.

Nice! Was that how he'd thought about all the time they'd spent together? The sweet intimacy they'd shared? It had just been—nice? And couldn't he have woken her and told her goodbye? Or had she not deserved that much from him?

Oh, Lord help her, she prayed. She wasn't sure she was going to make it through the day, much less the rest of her life.

"I'm not glum. Just trying to deal with these sniffles. And the ranch is quiet now. The whole crew is gone, including Matthew," she forced herself to say.

As Camille scooped up the eggs and slid them onto the plate, Peggy cast her a shrewd look. "I thought he was staying until the weekend. That's a bummer. He was going to come by the diner."

"Couldn't be helped. My brother, Blake, has come down with the flu and Matthew was needed back at Three Rivers," she explained, then thrust the plate of food at Peggy. "Here. Maybe this will make the customer happy. I gave them an extra egg—at no charge."

"I'll make sure to tell the woman," Peggy said, then hurried away with the food.

As soon as she disappeared from the kitchen, Edie stuck her head through the swinging doors. "What about my pancakes, Camille?"

"They're ready." She dumped crisp bacon atop the pancakes and handed it to the second waitress. "What time is it, anyway, Edie? It feels like I've been cooking breakfast food for hours."

The young blonde woman glanced at the watch on her wrist. "Nine thirty-five," she announced. "We ought to be getting close to the end of the breakfast run."

Edie hurried away with the pancakes, and seeing she was caught up for the moment, Camille sat down on the wooden stool and pressed a tissue to her running nose.

Nine thirty-five. She had no way of knowing when Matthew had left the house, but by now he'd had plenty of time to make the four-hour trip to Three Rivers. No doubt he was already back in the swing of giving orders to the men and dealing with whatever Blake needed to have done around the ranch.

He loved his job. It was his life. Just as this diner had become her life. She couldn't expect things to be any other way. So why was she having to fight like hell just to keep tears from rolling down her face?

Because she understood that this was nothing like being jilted by Graham Danby. The only thing she'd suffered over that incident was squashed pride. Her feelings for Matthew were deep and real. The kind that lived on in spite of time or distance.

Perhaps she'd made a mistake in not telling him that she loved him. But she didn't think so. Matthew had no desire to be a husband or father. He'd not been raised to embrace such roles in his life. And Renee's desertion had only reinforced his doubts about being a married man. No. He didn't want to hear about love. Not from her or any woman.

When Peggy returned to the kitchen, Camille was dabbing her seeping eyes with a napkin. The waitress shook her head with dismay and wrapped a comforting arm around Camille's shoulders.

"Oh honey, don't tell me you're crying because Matthew has gone home! Before he came you were dreading having to put up with the man!"

She sniffed and lowered the napkin from her eyes. "I'm not crying about Matthew," she said stubbornly.

"Sure you aren't. Just like Thanksgiving never falls on a Thursday," she said dryly. "Who are you trying to fool? Yourself?"

Camille dropped her head and mumbled, "No. I'm just teary-eyed because—well, things can't be the way I want them to be, that's all. I have my life here with the diner. And he has his on Three Rivers. It's as simple as that."

Peggy went over to the huge coffee urn and filled a cup. When she handed it to Camille, she said, "Doesn't sound simple at all to me. Unless you've come to the conclusion that the man is worth more than this place."

She waved her arm around the kitchen, and Camille shot her a droll look. "There's no question about it, Peggy. Matthew is worth a hundred diners. But it wouldn't do me any good to give up this place. That wouldn't make him fall in love with me."

"Is that what you believe? That he doesn't love you?"

"I don't just believe it, Peg, I know it. So the only choice I have is to stiffen my spine and get over him."

Peggy rolled her eyes. "Oh boy, now that might be easier said than done. From what I saw the other day, Matthew is one hunk of a man. Quiet. But sexy as heck. He'd make any woman's heart flutter."

And no doubt there were plenty of women back in Yavapai County who'd be more than happy to get a few hours of his company from time to time. The thought stirred nausea through the pit of Camille's stomach.

"There's a foolproof medicine to cure that kind of heart problem," Camille told her firmly.

Peggy's brows arched in question. "What's that? A double shot of Scotch?"

Camille put her tissue away and returned to the grill. "No. Hard work. And that's what I plan for all of us to be doing here at The Lost Antelope. The holidays are coming and I have all kinds of ideas to make them special for our customers."

"Holidays? Did someone mention the holidays?" Edie asked as she bounced into the room and handed Camille another breakfast order.

"I did," Camille answered as she slapped several thick slabs of bacon on the grill. "Why?"

"Because I think we should have a traditional turkey dinner with all the trimmings and give the meals away to anyone who wants one—uh, until the food runs out, that is."

Peggy was flabbergasted. "Give the dinners away! Camille just bought this place. She can't make money like that!"

Camille glanced over her shoulder at the two waitresses. "Edie, I think you have a great idea. It would be the perfect way to show the customers how much we appreciate them."

Grinning smugly, Edie patted the blue bandana tied over her head. "See, sometimes I'm more than a ditzy blonde."

Peggy let out a good-natured groan while Edie giggled, but Camille couldn't summon up anything more than a wan smile. Would she ever be able to laugh again? she wondered.

"Okay, genius," Peggy teased. "Better go warm up the customers' coffee or you're going to hear some loud grumbling out there."

Humming a happy tune, Edie grabbed up the coffee carafe and headed back to the dining room. Peggy walked over to Camille and gave her shoulder an encouraging squeeze.

"I understand you're feeling down right now. But aren't you the woman who told me she believes in miracles?" she asked.

Camille sighed. "Yes. But—"

"No buts," Peggy interrupted. "You either believe in miracles or you don't."

With that bit of advice, Peggy left the kitchen, and as Camille continued to cook the rest of the breakfast order, she realized that she had to believe a miracle would bring Matthew back to her. Otherwise, her hopes for a happy future were over.

Chapter Twelve

Thanksgiving turned out to be an exhausting work day for everyone at the diner, but it was a huge success with the customers. Camille decided she was on the right track with the idea of the blue plate special, and the following week she worked tirelessly to implement all the changes the diner needed before they could actually begin offering it on the menu.

By the middle of the following week, Camille could hardly put one foot in front of the other and she was struggling just to keep a few bites of food in her queasy stomach.

"I think you're coming down with that nasty flu bug, Camille," Gideon said as he placed a tub full of dirty coffee cups into the sudsy water. "And it's only going to get worse if you don't get yourself to the doctor."

"I don't have time for a doctor's appointment,

Gideon. Peggy can't cook and waitress at the same time. And Edie had to take off today to take her mom to the doctor. Seems the woman has the flu or something like it."

"See, that's what I'm telling you." Gideon pointed a dirty fork at her to emphasize his words. "Edie has probably carried the germs here to you. So go get your coat and head over to Benson to the doctor."

Camille glanced at the clock hanging on the wall above the double sink where Gideon was washing dishes. "It's two o'clock. The lunch customers have let up." She pondered for a moment. "Now might be a good time to go."

"That's right. If anyone shows up, I'll cook. It won't be as good as your stuff, but it'll be edible."

"All right," Camille reluctantly agreed. "I can't afford to get sick and miss work. And I sure don't want to spread a stomach virus through the diner."

"Now you're talking," Gideon said with a vigorous nod.

Peggy walked into the kitchen just as Camille was pulling off her apron.

"Talking about what?" Peggy asked, then cast a concerned look at Camille's pale face. "Honey, you look awful. Are you going home for the rest of the day?"

"She's going to the doctor," Gideon answered for Camille. "And high time, too."

Peggy didn't waste any time fetching Camille's coat and handbag from the little office off the kitchen.

As she helped her on with the coat, she said, "If the wait at the clinic turns out to be long, don't worry about the diner. Gideon and I will close up. I'll let him take the cash home."

Camille shook her head. "I'm coming straight back here no matter how late it is. I have to put in some food orders for next week's menu."

The wait at the clinic wasn't quite as long as Camille was anticipating. An hour and a half after she entered the medical building, she walked out in a mental fog.

She wasn't coming down with the flu or anything close to a virus. The family practitioner had pronounced her six weeks pregnant! She was going to have Matthew's baby!

With an appointment card to her regular gynecologist stuffed in her purse and a prescription for nausea, she climbed into the car and stuck the key into the ignition. But that was as far as she got.

For long moments, Camille was too stunned to do much more than stare blindly out the windshield at the people coming and going through the front entrance of the medical building. Never in her wildest dreams had she anticipated something like this. She'd been taking the Pill, yet here she was on her way to being a single mother!

It happens occasionally, the doctor had explained to her. But how was she going to explain that to Matthew? What was he going to think? That she'd deliberately misled him about the birth control?

No. She felt sure he knew her better than to think she'd been lying about something so important to both their lives. But she was also fairly certain that he had no plans to become a daddy. Not to Camille's child, or any other woman's child.

On the drive back to Dragoon, Camille tried to collect herself. But the minute she walked into the diner and looked at Gideon's and Peggy's concerned faces, she burst into tears.

Rushing to her side, Peggy clutched her arm. "Oh honey, what in the world?"

Gideon put down his dish towel and in fatherly fashion led Camille over to the step chair sitting at the end of the work counter.

After gently removing her coat and handing it and her handbag to Peggy, he urged Camille into the chair.

"Now, what are all these tears about?" he asked in a firm but caring voice. "Do you have something worse than the flu?"

Camille looked at Peggy's worried face, then up to Gideon's. "I'm not sick. The doctor says I'm as healthy as a horse."

Peggy cursed. "What kind of idiot did you see? I'm about as far away from being a doctor as you can get, but even I can see you're sick as a dog! You can't hold a thing on your stomach!"

Camille drew in a long breath, then blew it out. "That's because I'm pregnant."

Peggy and Gideon exchanged stunned glances.

"A baby?" Peggy asked in an awed voice. "Matthew's baby?"

Camille scowled at her. "Who else?"

Peggy spluttered. "Uh—sorry—I—didn't mean it like that! It's—well, I realize you'd gotten close to Matthew—I just didn't know you'd gotten *that* close."

Camille groaned and then another fresh spurt of tears streamed from her eyes.

Gideon shot Peggy an annoyed glare. "Peg, would it kill you to use a little more tact sometimes?"

The waitress rolled her eyes at him. "Tact isn't going to change the fact that Camille is going to have a baby!"

"She's right, Gideon," Camille said dully. "I don't expect to be coddled. And I sure don't want you two to have to tiptoe around the obvious. I had an affair with Matthew and because of it we're going to be parents. Or should I say, I'm going to be a parent."

Peggy and Gideon exchanged more strained glances before Gideon placed a hand on her shoulder. "Why do you say it like that, Camille? Don't you think your young man will want to be a father to the child?"

Would he? Yes. He'd been too hurt by his own father to ever let a child of his feel unloved and unwanted. Yet she couldn't see him having anything more than a long-distance relationship with his son or daughter.

"He'll be a father," Camille admitted. "Just not on a daily basis."

"Does that mean you're not going back to Three Rivers?" Peggy wanted to know.

Frowning, Camille shook her head. "The thought never entered my mind. My home is on Red Bluff. This diner is mine now. I'm not leaving. I'll be raising my child here."

Gideon didn't look a bit relieved. "But you are going to tell the man about the baby, aren't you? It wouldn't be right to keep it from him."

Camille dabbed a tissue to her eyes. "Yes, I'll be telling him. I just don't know how or when."

Peggy's pained expression suddenly transformed into a smile. "What are we all looking so glum about? You've wanted a baby of your own for a long time. Now you're going to have one! This should be a celebration!"

Gideon nodded in agreement. "Peggy has the right

idea now. This is a joyous occasion. We've already locked the front door for closing time. Let's have a toast with a beer."

"Gideon, what are you thinking? Camille can't have beer!" Peggy scolded him.

Recognizing his mistake, he snapped his fingers. "Oh shoot, that's right. Okay, let's have milkshakes. I'll make them."

Gideon left to go after the ice cream and Camille gave Peggy a half-hearted smile. "In spite of these tears, Peggy, I'm really happy about the baby. I already love it—more than anything."

"Well, sure you do, honey. And you're going to be the best of mothers." She gave Camille's shoulders a hug, then stepped back and eyed her curiously. "So, what do you think your family is going to say? Especially your mother?"

Camille shook her head. "I honestly can't say. Any other time Mom would be crying and laughing and hugging me with joy. But now—I'm not so sure. She's been so different this past year. And then there's the fact that she's very close to Matthew. She considers him her fifth son. I don't know what to expect from her or any of the family. I do know that I can't breathe a word of this to my mother or my siblings. Not until I talk with Matthew."

"And when do you plan on doing that? Tonight?"

Camille gasped. "Not hardly! I'm not yet ready to deal with him."

"You think putting it off is going to make it easier?" Peggy asked.

"No. But it will give me time to plan what I'm going to say to him." Like how she didn't expect anything from him. Like how she understood their time together was nothing but sex to him and therefore he had no emotional investment in her.

The thought put a hard lump of pain in her throat, but she did her best to swallow it away.

"You might just be surprised by Matthew's reaction to the baby," Peggy gently suggested. "He might be thrilled."

Camille's short laugh was a cynical sound. "Oh, Peggy, sometimes I think you should have been a stand-up comedian."

A week later the weather turned unusually cold for Yavapai County. Matthew and the men had been extra busy keeping a closer eye on the cattle and making sure none of the pumps at the watering tanks had frozen.

The Three Rivers Ranch house was decked out with Christmas decorations, and the festive season had carried over into the horse barn, where each stall was adorned with evergreen wreaths and bright red bows. Colorful lights blazed in the front yard and also decorated the patio in the back.

Christmas was always a joyful season at the ranch, and this year the Hollisters had been especially blessed with all the new little family members. Yet Matthew didn't have to wonder if one certain Hollister would be here for the holiday. He already knew that Camille would be at Red Bluff.

She had the diner to run. And even if she didn't, he could hardly imagine her wanting to drive up here to Three Rivers and be faced with her siblings and their families.

Inside the huge horse barn, Matthew and TooTall

were unsaddling the horses they'd ridden today when Matthew's phone dinged with a message.

He tossed the loosened breast collar over the seat of the saddle and pulled the phone from his jacket pocket.

The message was from Blake: Come by the office before you leave.

Across from him, TooTall asked, "You going to eat with us at the bunkhouse before you go home?"

Normally Matthew made a point of eating with the crew of men at least three or four times a week. The shared time gave him a chance to hear their ideas or grievances and let them see that he considered their feelings important. But tonight he wasn't in the mood for food or talk.

"I'm not really hungry, TooTall. And anyway, I've got to go by the office and see Blake."

The cowboy frowned. "You're getting as thin as a snake, Matthew. You need to eat."

He tried to eat, Matthew thought. But every time he sat down at the dinner table, he started thinking about all the meals Camille had prepared for him, and his throat would close up to the point that swallowing the smallest bite of anything was painful.

"I'll get something to eat when I get home," he told TooTall. "You don't need to be worried about me."

TooTall pulled the bridle from his horse, then tossed it over his shoulder before he turned and looked at Matthew. "Maybe no one else around here knows you're hurting. But I do."

The suggestive remark was the first one that TooTall had made to him since they'd come home from Red Bluff, and it caught Matthew by complete surprise.

"I don't know what you're talking about," he muttered. "And I don't want to know."

"You're not happy."

For the past few weeks since he and the men had returned to Three Rivers, Matthew had been careful to behave as though nothing had changed with him. He'd been determined not to let anyone suspect that he was dying inside. But TooTall was a different matter. It was like the man could see right through a person.

Jerking loose the leather cinch strap, Matthew mindlessly wrapped it through the keeper on the saddle. "What would you know about it?"

"I know you don't belong here anymore," TooTall told him. "You know it, too. That's why you're unhappy."

Damn. Damn. Damn.

He scowled at the cowboy. "Do you know how mad you make me when you start this nonsense?"

TooTall shook his head. "Not mad at me. At yourself."

Matthew wasn't going to argue with the man. For one thing, he didn't have the energy. Nor did he have the heart for it.

"I suppose you've been having more of those visions," Matthew grumbled.

"No. They only come to me once in a while. Like when my mother died."

TooTall turned back to his horse and Matthew felt even worse than he had before. Like him, TooTall had endured a tough childhood, and both men had lost their mothers at a very young age. They each understood what the other had gone through and the connection had bonded them in a way that was more than mere friendship.

"Damn it, TooTall, I'm sorry," he said gruffly. "You're right. I am miserable. But there's nothing I can do about it."

The cowboy glanced over his shoulder at Matthew. "A way will come. You'll see."

Matthew wasn't going to bother asking him what he meant by that. Instead, he finished caring for his horse and walked over to the cattle barn to see Blake.

Inside the office, Flo was still at her desk. She looked up at Matthew, then quickly motioned him toward the door that opened to Blake's office.

"He's in there."

"And you're obviously burning the midnight oil," Matthew said to the woman. "Isn't it time for you to go home?"

She shrugged. "I don't have anything there except a spoiled cat and a TV. They can wait."

Matthew gave her a dismissive wave, then entered Blake's office. The man was on the phone, so Matthew used the time to pour himself a cup of the syrupy black coffee that had been left over from earlier in the day.

By the time Matthew made himself comfortable in one of the padded chairs in front of Blake's desk, the other man tossed the receiver of the landline back on its hook.

"Damned hay grower! Just because we're headed into winter, he thinks that gives him reason to price-gouge us ranchers. Well, I've got news for him. I can get it shipped in from California cheaper than what he's asking."

Matthew took a careful sip of the coffee, then grimaced at the taste of the gritty liquid. "This stuff could probably run a diesel for twenty miles."

"Sorry. Flo thinks she's above making coffee for me and I've been too busy." Linking his hands at the back of his neck, he stretched, then leaned back in his executive chair. "Have you seen the weather forecast?"

"No. We've been checking cattle all afternoon and my phone didn't have a signal until we got back here to the ranch yard. Why? Is it supposed to get colder?"

"Worse than that. Snow is being predicted for the southern part of the state. I'm worried about the calves at Red Bluff."

Red Bluff. Just hearing the ranch's name caused his insides to twist into unbearable knots.

Shaking his head, Matthew repeated the key word. "Snow? I don't believe that for a minute. It would be a cold day in hell before snow fell at Red Bluff."

Blake thoughtfully rubbed a hand along his jaw. "I wouldn't say that. I remember Dad talking about snow down there years ago."

"Years ago isn't now. You're worrying for nothing."

"I'm not worrying, but I am going to be cautious. That's why I'm sending you back down there. If it does snow I want you to make sure the cows can get their calves to some sort of shelter. There's four men already down there. If you—"

Matthew felt as though his whole body was turning to a chunk of ice. "No! There's no need for me to go to Red Bluff, Blake. You're making a mountain out of a molehill."

Blake stared at him as if he'd lost his mind, and Matthew figured he had gone a little crazy. Just the thought of seeing Camille again, of hearing her voice, touching her and then saying goodbye all over again, was too much for him to bear.

"What the hell has come over you, Matthew? It isn't like you to argue about something like this. In fact, it isn't like you to argue at all!"

Rising from the chair, Matthew walked over to the large picture window behind Blake's desk. Beyond the glass he could see a portion of the ranch yard and a cluster of smaller barns and corrals illuminated by security lights. This had been his home, his life for so many years, he could find his way through the maze in the blackest of nights. And yet it was like TooTall had said. Matthew didn't belong here anymore. Not when his heart was elsewhere.

"Sorry, Blake. I realize you have enough problems on your hands without me adding to them. But—I—don't want to go to Red Bluff. It's that simple."

"Simple." He repeated the word softly as though it was something foreign coming out of Matthew's mouth. "That's right! I give you a simple order and you act as though I'm asking you to march into a war zone without a weapon to defend yourself! I don't understand you, Matthew. And now that we're speaking frankly, I'll just come out and say it—I'm worried about you. You look awful and you're acting even worse and—"

"Okay, Blake," he interrupted harshly. "I'll tell you what's wrong. I don't want to go back to Red Bluff because—of Camille."

When Blake didn't immediately reply, he turned to see the man was staring at him in stunned silence. "Camille? I don't understand. Did you two get into it about something while you were down there?"

Matthew felt his face turn as hot as a furnace. "No.

It's not anything like that, Blake. You see, I did something stupid while I was down at Red Bluff. I—uh, fell in love with your sister."

Blake's eyes narrowed to shrewd slits and Matthew braced himself for the worst. Yet instead of the man spewing out a long tirade about betrayal and misconduct, a wide smile spread across his face.

Finally, he said, "Well, thank God. I was afraid something was really wrong with you."

Groaning, Matthew lifted his hat and shoved a hand through his hair as though the act would clear his jumbled brain. "What are you talking about, Blake? Something *is* really wrong!"

The misery in Matthew's voice turned Blake's smile into a concerned frown.

"Why?" he asked. "Camille isn't interested?"

Once again Matthew felt like a torch had passed over his face. "What do you mean—interested?"

Blake shook his head in disbelief, then followed that with a chuckle. "Okay, let me put it this way—does she like you?"

Like? After all that he'd shared with Camille, the word seemed downright silly. But how, exactly, did she feel about him?, Matthew wondered for the umpteenth time. True, she'd made it very clear that she enjoyed his company in bed and even out of it. But she'd never talked about love or said that she might want him in her life for the long haul.

"Well, yes. She likes me. I mean—we got along fine. Really fine."

"Then what's the problem?" Blake questioned. "Seems to me if you're that crazy about the woman you'd be jumping at the chance to go to Red Bluff."

Unable to look the man in the face, Matthew rested his hip on the corner of Blake's desk and stared at the intricate design on the tiled floor. "I don't want to go—because it hurts too much. I'll—" He drew in a long breath and blew it out. "After a few days I'll have to leave again and that's not an easy thing to do."

Somewhere inside him, he found the courage to look Blake in the eye. "Can you imagine driving away from Katherine and not knowing if, or when, you might see her again?"

Sudden dawning passed over Blake's handsome face, followed by a wealth of compassion. "You really do love my sister," he said gently.

Matthew nodded. "I didn't want to. It just happened."

"Yeah. It's something a man can't stop." Blake's perceptive gaze continued to study Matthew's face. "So what are you going to do about it?"

"There's not much I can do. She's made a life for herself there. I couldn't ask her to leave it. I know what that's like, Blake. Renee did it to me and—I resented it like hell—and that's when I knew it was over between us. I'm not about to do that to Camille."

Blake remained thoughtful. "Sounds like you're in a mess. Does she know how you feel about her?"

Matthew gave him a noncommittal shrug. "I think she does."

"Think! Man, you can't just let a woman wonder about such things! That's dangerous!"

Matthew was amazed that Blake couldn't fully comprehend the situation. Telling Camille how he felt wasn't going to change anything. It was only going to make matters far more miserable.

Matthew walked over to a wastebasket and tossed away the foam cup and bitter coffee. "So you say."

From his seat behind the desk, Blake continued to watch him, and Matthew got the feeling the man was calculating something. He just couldn't imagine what it might be.

"Matthew, are you afraid Camille might not be over Graham Danby?"

I want to laugh until my sides hurt.

Camille's words suddenly waltzed through his mind and he barked out a loud laugh. "Not in the least."

Blake shot him an odd look, then said, "Okay. I want you to go pack your bags and head to Red Bluff in the morning. And I expect you to stay until the weather clears. Got it?"

"Yeah. I got it. I'm just going to ask one thing of you. Can I take TooTall with me?"

Blake gave him a single nod. "I'll call him right now and let him know to be ready."

Matthew started to the door.

Behind him, Blake added, "And Matthew, things have a way of working out. So no more worrying about anything. Hear me?"

Hardly encouraged, Matthew nodded and left the office.

Chapter Thirteen

Camille stood in the middle of the living room of the Red Bluff hacienda and surveyed the Christmas decorations she'd been slowly putting up this past week. Red, pink and white poinsettias adorned the tables and flanked the hearth of the fireplace, while on a wall table, she'd erected a small nativity scene complete with wise men, shepherds and barn animals. In front of the window overlooking the back courtyard, a tall pine was covered with twinkling lights, sparkling tinsel, bows and ornaments of all colors, and a pretty angel sitting on the highest bough. The festive tree gave her a measure of comfort, but it couldn't take away the dark doubts weighing on her shoulders.

Today she'd come to the conclusion that she couldn't put off seeing Matthew any longer. Christmas was rapidly approaching and before the parties at Three Rivers began in earnest and The Lost Antelope was jammed with holiday travelers, she needed to make a trip to Yavapai County and give Matthew the news about the coming baby.

Since her fiasco of an engagement with Graham had ended more than two years ago, Camille hadn't stepped foot on Three Rivers. For the first few months after she'd left the ranch, she'd been afraid to go back, afraid to face her family and the failure of being unable to hold on to her fiancé. However, it hadn't taken her long to see that sort of thinking was ludicrous. Graham hadn't been worth a second thought. Besides, everyone failed at something at some point in their life.

But this thing with Matthew was a whole different matter. She loved him with all her heart and she was going to have his baby. Even if he didn't want to be in their lives on a daily basis, she wanted him to know how she felt about him, and about the baby they'd created together. She could go back to Three Rivers for all those reasons.

Squaring her shoulders, she climbed the stairs to her bedroom and pulled out a pair of suitcases from beneath the bed.

Both of them were nearly filled with the clothes and toiletries she thought she'd need for the short stay, when her cell phone rang.

Moving over to the nightstand, she picked up the phone, and then, seeing the name of the caller, promptly placed it back on the tabletop. Ever since elementary school, Emily-Ann had been her best friend, and normally she would be happy to chat with her. But the two of them had always shared their ups and downs with each other. Camille feared that once she started talking she wouldn't be able to quit. She'd end up telling her about Matthew and the baby, and Camille couldn't risk the chance of him getting the news from anyone other than herself. Not that Emily-Ann was a gossiper, but things slipped out accidentally sometimes.

The phone stopped ringing and Camille went back to her packing. But less than two minutes later, it started ringing again. Only this time the caller wasn't Emily-Ann. It was Peggy.

Camille quickly answered it. "Peg, I'm glad you called because I needed to talk to you about the diner."

"Well, I'm calling about the diner, too," the woman explained. "Edie needs off in the morning, so I told her I'd fill in for her. If that's okay with you."

Camille sank onto the edge of the bed. "It's okay. It just means that Gideon will have to help you cook."

"Me and Gideon cooking together, oh Lord. That's going to be fun. Uh—why, are you too sick to come in or something?"

"I'm feeling okay. But I'm going to take off for a day or two—three at the most. Do you think you and Gideon can handle the place? If Edie is going to be off for very long—"

"No. She only need a couple of hours in the morning. Otherwise, she'll be at work. But why do you need to take off? Are you keeping something from me, Camille? Is something wrong with the baby?"

"No. No. Quit worrying. I've decided to drive up to Three Rivers and tell Matthew about the baby."

"Oh."

"Yes. Oh. And I want to get it done and over with before Christmas."

"That's a good idea, Camille," Peggy replied. "You're doing the right thing."

Camille pinched the bridge of her nose and willed away the tears that were always near the surface of her emotions. "I know, Peg. It's just going to be—difficult. And not only with seeing Matthew, but facing my whole family. They're all going to be whispering that little Camille has messed up again."

"Who says you've messed up? I don't."

From Peggy's standpoint, Camille was blessed. Husband or not, she was going to have a child of her own. "Well, you're just a bit biased, Peggy. But thanks for your support."

"So, when are you leaving for Three Rivers?" Peggy asked.

Camille answered, "As early in the morning as possible."

"That might be wise, to get up there before the weather turns bad," Peggy advised. "I keep hearing we're going to get snow or possibly freezing rain in our area. Can you believe it?"

"I'll believe it when I see it. But say a little prayer for me anyway. The last thing I want is to get stranded on a slick highway."

"I'll say two prayers for you, Camille. For safe, clear driving and for good luck with Matthew."

"Thanks, Peggy. As far as Matthew is concerned, I'm going to need that miracle we've talked about."

The two women talked a few more minutes about the diner and then ended the call.

Camille went to work finishing her packing, but before she zipped the lid shut on the last case, she fetched a little Christmas angel from the nightstand and dropped it among the folded clothing.

The next morning before daylight, Camille jumped out of bed as soon as the alarm went off, but she didn't get the early start she'd been planning on. As soon as her feet touched the floor, nausea hit her in giant waves.

After fetching a few crackers from the kitchen, she lay back down in the bed and slowly munched on the dry food in hopes it would settle her roiling stomach.

By the time sunshine was beginning to peek through the curtains on the window, she'd eaten the crackers and to her great relief was feeling well enough to get up and dress.

She was about to remove her robe when she heard a faint rattling noise that sounded very much like a stock trailer going by the house. Which would be strange, she thought. At this time of the year, Blake didn't purchase or sell cattle, nor did he move them from one place to the other. So why was a trailer being used at this early hour in the morning?

Telling herself that the comings and goings of the ranch hands were hardly her business, she reached for the jeans she'd laid out to wear when a faint knock sounded on the kitchen door at the back of the house.

Annoyed at the interruption, she tossed the jeans back onto the bed and, tying the sash of her robe back around her waist, she hurried downstairs and out to the kitchen.

Before she managed to reach the door, the knock sounded again, only longer this time. With an impatient shake of her head, she called out, "Just a minute. I'm coming!"

Flinging her tousled hair back off her face, she unbolted the door and pulled it open, then nearly fainted.

"Matthew!" His name was all she could manage as she stared at him in stunned fascination. He was wearing his normal work clothes, only this morning his shirt was covered with a brown canvas jacket. The dark leather collar was turned up against his neck and the brim of his gray hat was pulled low over his forehead. Cold wind had left his skin splotched with red.

"Hello, Camille."

Her mind whirling with a storm of questions, she pushed the door wide and gestured for him to come in.

He stepped into the kitchen and she shut the door against the freezing air whooshing in behind him.

He said, "I—uh—guess you're wondering what I'm doing here."

Clamping her trembling hands together, she turned to face him. "Since I've not talked to Blake, I have no idea why you're here."

He grimaced, and as Camille's gaze slipped over him, she thought he looked gaunt and just a bit haggard. The idea that he might've been ill sent fear spiraling through her. Even though the man was breaking her heart, she wanted him to be healthy and happy and safe. That was the true meaning of loving someone. And she truly loved Matthew.

"The weather," he said.

When he didn't explain further, she looked at him blankly. "Uh—what about the weather? Other than it's cold for Cochise County."

"And it's going to get colder. It might even snow. So Blake sent me down to watch over the cattle for the next few days. If worse comes to worst we might have to herd as many as we can into the barns."

She released the pent-up breath she hadn't realized she'd been holding until now. "Oh, I see. Peggy mentioned something to me last night about snow. I honestly didn't take her seriously."

"It's serious. Otherwise, I wouldn't be here."

She practically flinched at that, but managed to keep a stoic look on her face as she turned and walked over to the cabinet. "I'd offer you some coffee, but I've not made any yet. I'm running late this morning."

"I need to get down to the barn anyway and help TooTall unload the horses."

"Okay." She glanced over her shoulder to see him wiping a gloved hand over his face. Just looking at him made her ache to throw herself into his arms. "Uh— while you're here, will you be staying in the house?"

"The bunkhouse is full," he said. "But if my being in the house bothers you, I can probably wedge another cot in somewhere."

Were they crazy? Camille wondered. They were talking to each other like two strangers awkwardly trying to communicate in different languages.

Marching back over to where he stood, she frowned at him. "It's a little late to be worrying about something like that now, don't you think?"

"Camille, I don't have time to discuss sleeping arrangements right now! I—"

It was all she could do to keep from slapping his face. "I'll bet you don't," she muttered. "Just like you didn't have the time or the courtesy to wake me and tell me goodbye."

His face turned a sickening gray color. "I had my reasons for leaving like I did."

"Sure you did. The main one being that you're a coward!"

His jaw grew tight and then he looked away from her. "You're right," he said stiffly. "When it comes to you and me, I'm a big coward."

She wasn't exactly sure what he meant by that and trying to figure it out could wait until later, she thought. Right now, there was something far more important on her mind.

"Matthew, maybe you're curious as to why I'm not already at the diner this morning. And maybe you're not. But I'll explain it anyway. I was planning to leave in a few minutes for Three Rivers."

She had never seen him looking so shocked, or seen so many questions swirling in his gray eyes.

"Three Rivers! I don't believe it!"

She could understand his disbelief. Like him, she'd been a coward for far too long. But she was well and truly over that now. "If you don't believe me, go look in my car. My bags are already loaded in the back seat."

His lips parted. "But why? It's still a few weeks before Christmas," he said, and then his eyes suddenly narrowed. "Does your family know you're going up there?"

She shook her head. "No. Seeing them wasn't my main reason for going. And now that you're here there's no need for me to go at all."

He looked confused and suspicious at the same time. "Why?"

"Because you're the one I was really going to see."

"Me?"

She nodded, and as luck would have it, a pang of

queasiness shot through her stomach. Her hand un-wittingly pressed against her abdomen as she fought against the urge to rush over to the sink and throw up all the crackers she'd eaten.

"Yes, you," she said hoarsely. "I thought you needed to know that you're going to be a daddy."

His eyes grew wide and then his jaw dropped. "Are you saying—are you telling me that—"

Nodding, she said, "Yes, I'm pregnant. In roughly seven and a half months you'll be more than Three Rivers's fore-man. You'll be the father of a Hollister baby."

The sickly gray color of his face was suddenly blotched with spots of bright color. Other than the changes in his complexion, his face was a mask, making it impossible to determine what he was thinking.

"How long have you known?" he asked quietly.

"Only a few days. I never suspected I was pregnant. I was on the Pill and thought it was impossible for me to conceive. But I've been so sick I had to go to the doctor to find out what was wrong," she explained.

"Sick? Are you all right now?"

His hands curved over the tops of her shoulders and it was all Camille could do to keep from flinging herself into his arms and sobbing out how much she loved him. But she should've done that weeks ago, before he left Red Bluff, she thought miserably. Now it would look far too convenient and contrived to start talking about love.

"Not exactly," she answered. "I'm having a heck of a bout of morning sickness right this minute."

"Oh." He let out a heavy breath and then, taking her by the arm, led her over to one of the chairs at the kitchen table.

Camille took a seat, and he walked over to the sink

and tore off several paper towels. After he'd wet them in cold water he carried them back to her.

"Here," he said. "Wipe your face. It might help."

She did as he suggested, then pulled in several deep breaths before she turned her attention back to him. As she watched him tug off his gloves and remove his hat, Camille decided he actually looked sicker than she was. Undoubtedly, he was still in a state of shock over the news.

He laid the items on the tabletop, then assessed her with a piercing look. "What do you think your family is going to say about this—about the baby?"

"I don't have to wonder about that, Matthew. They'll be very happy for me."

"And what about you?" he questioned, his face still an unreadable mask. "How do you feel about it?"

His stilted questions were annoying the heck out of her. This wasn't the Matthew she knew. Or the Matthew she'd fallen in love with. This man was as cold and stiff as a board out on the cattle barn. Had learning he was going to be a father done this to him? Or had the past weeks he'd been back at Three Rivers made him forget every tender moment they'd shared together?

"How do you think?" She shot the question back at him, and then, with a rueful sigh, added in a softer voice, "I'm in love with this baby. Totally and completely in love with it."

"Then that's all I need to know. Tomorrow we're going to drive down to Bisbee and get married at the courthouse," he told her in no uncertain terms. "I want this child to have legal, legitimate parents."

Camille stared at him while the pain lancing through her chest made her forget all about the upheaval in her stomach. No words of love. No proposal of marriage. Or vows to be at her side for the rest of his life. This had to be the coldest, cruelest thing he or any man could ever say to her.

"Matthew Waggoner, no man is going to *tell* me I'm going to marry him. And that includes you! As far as I'm concerned, you can forget about me and this baby. You can go right back to Three Rivers and stay there—it's where you belong!"

Her outburst momentarily stunned him and then his face turned colder than a piece of granite. Was this the same man who'd held her so tenderly in his arms? The man who'd brushed her hair and whispered sweet words in her ear? It couldn't be, she thought sickly.

His jaw tight, he said, "In case you've forgotten, I was sent down here to do a job. And I'm not leaving until it's done. So until then, you'll just have to put up with me." He jerked on his hat and gloves and stalked to the door. "Maybe you're the one who ought to run back to Three Rivers, Camille. That's what you want to do when trouble pops up, isn't it? Run and hide?"

She glanced around for something to throw at him and realized there wasn't anything close enough to get her hands on. "I must have been out of my mind to think you could deal with this in a sensitive way!"

His brows arched in sardonic fashion. "Sensitive? If that's what you want you should've tried to hold on to Graham Danby. Not go to bed with a cowboy!"

Her teeth clamped together. "I can tell you what I don't want, Matthew, and that's you!"

Late that afternoon as Matthew and TooTall rode their horses back to the ranch, fat flakes of snow began to fall from the high ceiling of gray clouds. The sight of the ominous weather didn't surprise him. It seemed everything today was supposed to go from bad to worse.

"Look, Yellow Hair, the ground is already turning white," TooTall exclaimed as he turned up the collar of his old plaid coat and hunched down in the saddle. "I hope those mama cows in the south pastures have sense enough to take their babies to the bluff. That's the only decent shelter on that range."

"Hope is the best we can do for now. It's so far to that section of the ranch, it would be dark by the time we reached the herd. First thing in the morning we'll head down there."

Tugging the brim of his hat lower on his forehead, Matthew peered through the falling snow toward the ranch yard and the house beyond. Whether Camille would be home whenever he got there was questionable, but one way or the other they had to talk tonight. And not like a pair of sparring birds, warily circling each other, but like two adults with a baby to consider.

He'd never been so blindsided in his life when she'd told him she was pregnant. And now that he'd had several hours to think about it, he had to admit that a huge part of him was thrilled to the very core of his being. He'd never thought he would be a father, and to think the woman he loved more than anything was going to bear his child was incredible. Even if she didn't want him as a husband, the connection to her was more profound than anything he'd ever expected to have.

"How was Camille this morning?" TooTall asked. "You never said."

It had taken Matthew most of the day to absorb the

news about the baby, much less talk to anyone else about it.

"She was kinda sickly."

TooTall grunted. "That's the way it is for a woman. She goes through a lot for a man."

Matthew's head jerked over to the cowboy riding by his side. "How did you—"

"I had a—"

"Vision," Matthew finished before TooTall could get the last word out. "Sometimes, TooTall, I wish you'd keep these things to yourself!"

The other man didn't bother to look in Matthew's direction. "And sometimes I wish I didn't see them," he retorted, then cast Matthew a wry look. "Don't fret. It's all going to be good, Matthew."

Good, hell! Camille was carrying his child and she didn't want to marry him. Just mentioning the word marriage to her had sent her into a furious frenzy. But then, he should've expected that. He was a Waggoner and she was a Hollister. Such things didn't happen. Not in his world.

Camille rapidly counted the stack of bills in her hand and placed them on the desk along with the remainder of the money the diner had taken in for the day. Because of the worsening weather, she'd decided to close up an hour early to give Peggy and Gideon plenty of time to drive home before dark. As for herself, she was dreading the idea of going to Red Bluff and facing Matthew tonight.

"Everything is shut down," Peggy announced as she stuck her head in the open door to the office. "And

Gideon has already left. He wanted me to remind you to drive carefully on the way to the ranch."

Camille glanced over to see Peggy had already pulled on her coat and tugged a sock cap over her black hair.

"I would be more than grateful, Peg, if you'd let me bunk in your spare bedroom for the next few days. Just until Matthew leaves."

Frowning, Peggy stepped into the room that looked spacious and neat since Camille had cleaned out Norman's clutter. "Of course you're welcome to stay at my place. You didn't even have to ask. But don't you think you're being a little hasty? And a bit stubborn?"

Camille whirled the swivel chair around so that she was facing her friend. "No! The man doesn't want a wife. All he wants is to give the baby two parents—legally bound by a piece of paper!"

Peggy made a palms-up gesture. "Isn't that what married people are?"

"Yes, but that's not enough. Not for me. The man demanded that I marry him! Demanded! How do you think that would make you feel?"

Peggy looked at her for a moment and then rolled with laughter. "Listen, Camille, if a man like Matthew ever demanded that I marry him, I'd think I was dreaming. And I probably would be. But one way or the other, I'd be standing in front of the altar letting him slip a ring on my finger."

Camille groaned with frustration, then dropped her face into both hands. "I don't want him that way."

"I thought you'd gotten over all that wounded pride business you were suffering from when you first came down here. What are you going to do? Let it take over again and ruin everything with Matthew? Okay, so he didn't approach the matter in a romantic way, but give him time. He's probably still in shock."

Dropping her hands from her face, Camille began to stuff the counted bills into a money bag. "Nothing shocks Matthew. That's what my father understood about him all those years ago. He realized that Matthew had the cool demeanor that would stand well as foreman of Three Rivers. And that hasn't changed—he's cool under the worst of conditions."

"You're talking about work now," Peggy reasoned. "I have a feeling this matter with you and the baby is very different for him."

The lump in her throat made it nearly impossible to speak. "Oh, Peg, maybe I am behaving childishly, but I—I don't think it's wrong for me to want real love from Matthew. Yet that's only a part of it. I'm very afraid that he might think I purposely got pregnant to trap him."

"Oh, Camille, that old ruse doesn't fit you at all. Matthew should be able to see that."

Maybe, Camille thought drearily. But she was the one who'd assured him that a pregnancy couldn't happen and he'd trusted her. Now she felt as though she'd betrayed him in some way. Which was even more stupid of her. No matter how much protection was being used, any time a man had sex with a woman he was running the risk of creating a child.

"I don't know anything anymore," she said miserably.

Peggy patted her shoulder. "You're not going to figure everything out about the baby and Matthew sitting here in this office. Let's get out of here and go home before the roads get too slick to travel."

Pushing herself up from the desk chair, Camille grabbed up her handbag, the day's take and her coat.

Peggy was right. She needed to get home to Red Bluff. She needed to face Matthew all over again. And this time she was going to make it clear to him that she wanted a marriage proposal spoken from his heart. She wanted his love. Nothing less would do.

Chapter Fourteen

When Matthew finally returned to the ranch house, it was dark and snow had covered everything in the courtyard, including the lounge chairs sitting under the branches of a Joshua tree.

It seemed like months had passed since he and Camille had lain together on one of the loungers. The stars had been bright that night and her kisses had been as hot as a red pepper baked in the sun. And later that evening, when he'd taken her to bed, she'd not hesitated to show him how much she'd wanted him.

But those times were over, he thought ruefully. This morning, she'd made it perfectly clear that she wanted nothing to do with him. Is that what having a baby did to a woman? Caused her feelings, her whole personality to take a one-hundred-eighty-degree turn? If so, Matthew didn't know how the Hollister men had endured their pregnant wives.

Except for a night-light over the gas range, the kitchen was dark. There were no delicious smells of cooking food or a smiling Camille setting the table for two. There was no kiss to greet him or promises of loving him through the night.

That idyllic time in his life had ended the morning he'd driven back to Three Rivers. And understanding that he'd never have the chance to regain those days again had made the long trip even more devastating for Matthew. But that didn't mean he was going to let her move completely move out of his life. Not with his baby. No, it was his child, too, and he wasn't going to be bashful about reminding her of the fact.

Still bundled in his hat and coat, he walked through to the living room, only to find Camille wasn't there, either. One small lamp illuminated a portion of the large space, and as his gaze took in the Christmas decorations and pine tree loaded with ornaments, a heavy weight of regret fell over him. They should be spending the holiday together, he thought, and celebrating the news that she was pregnant. Instead, she didn't want him near her.

Deciding she had to be in her bedroom, he climbed the stairs and entered through the partially opened door. After three steps into the room, he stopped and looked over to where she was standing at the side of the bed. An open suitcase was lying in front of her and one by one, she was folding pieces of clothing and stacking them carefully inside the case. The sight angered and sickened him at the same time.

Striding to her side, he asked, "What are you doing?"

She didn't make the effort to look at him. Instead, she stared at the inside of the suitcase and spoke stiffly, "That question is rather irrelevant, isn't it? I'm packing more of my things to go with what's already loaded in the car. I'm not going to stay another night in this house. I thought I could—I thought I could force myself. But you've ruined everything I ever loved about Red Bluff!"

Her last words snapped something inside him and before he could stop himself, he closed the lid on the suitcase and shoved it aside. Then, wrapping a hand around her upper arm, he turned her toward him.

"Forget the packing," he ordered gruffly. "You're not going anywhere! Snow is still falling out there and I'm not about to let you get on the highway and put yourself and our baby in danger! Just because you've decided you don't want me around anymore!"

Her mouth fell open and for long moments she studied him with wide, wondrous eyes. And then suddenly, as if a switch had been flipped, her features softened and her hands were clutching his forearms.

Lifting her chin to a challenging angle, she asked, "Why should my driving on a snowy road worry you, Matthew?"

He muttered an impatient curse under his breath. "That's a stupid question. It should be obvious to you!"

"There's nothing stupid about it. Or obvious. You wouldn't order anyone else to stay off the road. So why order me?" she persisted, while her fingers tightened their hold on his arms. "You have a mouth. Tell me."

If he'd been standing there naked he wouldn't have felt any more exposed than he did at this moment. Something inside of him was crumbling away like a weathered brick wall. And as it fell, it was revealing every emotion, every fear and doubt he'd carried around in his heart.

"I don't—damn it, Camille, if something happened

to you or our baby I couldn't bear it—because I love you. I've loved you for a long, long time. I just didn't recognize it until these past few weeks. Or maybe I did recognize it, but I didn't have the courage to really face my feelings head on."

She closed her eyes, but tears leaked onto her cheeks anyway. "Oh, Matthew, why didn't you tell me? That's all I needed to know. That's all I've ever wanted from you."

He pulled her close and buried his face in the curve of her neck. She smelled like lily of the valley and the scent evoked all the tender moments they'd shared in the past and would hopefully share in the future.

"You were right this morning when you called me a coward, Camille. All this time—all these years I've been afraid to admit my feelings for you—even to myself."

She eased his head back and smiled into his eyes. "But why, Matthew? If I'd only known I—"

He cradled her face between his hands. "You're a Hollister, Camille. I've never been good enough for you. I'm not sure I am now. But I have to believe that I am—because I can't let you go. Not now, or ever."

Shaking her head, she slipped her arms around his waist and drew herself closer. "I thought—for a long time I had this idea that you didn't like me. That you considered me nothing more than a shallow, spoiled brat. But that didn't stop me from thinking you were the grandest thing to ever walk on Three Rivers soil."

The sound coming out of him was something between a groan and a laugh. "If I'd only known."

More tears rolled down her cheeks, only this time they were a sign of great relief. "We've both been fools, Matthew! If we'd had the courage to be honest with each other, just think of all the misery we would've been spared. You with Renee and me with Graham." She pressed her cheek to his. "But that's all in the past. And I don't ever intend to let you go, either."

He eased her head back and slowly searched her face. "This morning you made it pretty damned clear you didn't want to marry me."

Laughing now, she kissed his cheeks and chin and finally his lips. "I was mad as fire at you, Matthew. I wanted you to *ask* me to marry you, not demand it. I wanted to hear you say that you loved me and wanted me to be your wife—that you'd love me for as long as you lived."

He swept off his hat and tossed it onto the bed, then went down on one knee in front of her. "I love you, Camille, more than anything. Will you be my wife? Will you give me this baby, and more babies, and stick by my side until the end of our days?"

She went down on her knees in front of him and wrapped her arms around his neck. "Yes, Matthew! Yes, to all those things! But first there's something I need to know."

Still uncertain, he asked, "What's that? About Three Rivers? The Lost Antelope?"

Shaking her head, she smiled at him. "No. We'll figure all that out later. I just need to know what you think about the baby and if you think I deliberately got pregnant to snare you."

A puzzled frown pulled his brows together. "Deliberate? It never crossed my mind, Camille. Not once."

Her eyes were suddenly glowing with so much love it practically took his breath away. "Oh, Matthew, I can't explain it. And the doctor told me a baby can't always be explained—it just happens."

"Yeah, if you're lucky," he said softly. "And right now I have to say I'm the luckiest guy on earth."

She pressed several kisses upon his lips, then hastily began to shove off his coat that was damp from the melting snowflakes.

After she'd tossed it aside, he took her by the hands and drew the both of them to a standing position.

As he began to undress her, she kissed him fervently, her lips conveying how much she'd missed him and how much she loved and wanted him. Now that he knew the feelings that were cradled in her heart, it made everything different for Matthew. And when they were finally on the bed and he was inside her, he thought he would die from the incredible pleasure pouring through him.

A long while later, Camille and Matthew lay cuddled together beneath the warm covers and watched the snow falling beyond the bedroom window.

"I hate to think of the little calves out in this weather," she said wistfully. "But I always try to remember what Daddy used to say—Mother Nature has a way of protecting them."

"Joel was right. And I don't believe the snow will get all that deep. Tomorrow we'll spend the day making sure none of them are stuck in drifts." He rubbed his chin against the top of her head. "This evening, while we were riding back to the ranch, TooTall told me that everything with me and you was going to turn out good. I didn't believe him."

"Really? How did he know?"

"He always knows. He's Yavapai and very mystical. He knew about our baby even before I did."

Completely bemused, she raised up on her elbow and smiled down at him. "Seriously?"

Matthew nodded. "Sometimes he has visions. His mother died when he was just a little boy. Like me. I guess you could say there's a bond between us that's different from what I have with the other men."

"That's understandable." She gently pushed her fingers through his tousled curls. "Did TooTall happen to mention what the baby's sex was?"

Matthew chuckled softly, then lifted his gaze up to her face. "No. But he did talk about Red Bluff and how I would be staying here. He even made me promise to make him my ramrod. I went along just to ease his mind. But all the while I was thinking this guy is slipping off the beam."

Her eyes full of questions, she asked, "And now?"

"Now I can see how right he was about everything. I do belong here on Red Bluff, Camille. This is where you're happy and I'm happy. It's where we need to raise our children and live out our lives. I don't want you to give up The Lost Antelope. Not for me or any reason."

Her head swung back and forth. "But I don't want you to give up Three Rivers just to make me happy."

"Oh, my little darling, Red Bluff is a part of Three Rivers. And Blake and Maureen have already been planning on turning it into a larger, full-time operation. Who do you think is going to run the place for them if I don't? Together, TooTall and I will turn this ranch into the jewel of Cochise County."

Sighing with contentment, she leaned down and kissed him. "I've never been so happy."

He took her by the shoulders and pressed her down on the pillow. "I want you to stay right here until I get back." He pulled the cover up to her armpits, then climbed out of bed and reached for his clothes.

"Where are you going?" she wanted to know.

He grinned at her. "This time I'm going to cook something for you and the baby. A cowboy can cook, you know—for the woman he loves."

Her joyous laughter followed him all the way down the stairs.

Epilogue

Several weeks later, on Christmas Eve, the hacienda on Red Bluff was ablaze with lights on the inside, while on the outside, decorative lights adorned the lawn and the back courtyard. Not only was the holiday being celebrated, but this evening the last Hollister sibling had married the man of her dreams.

Inside the living room, baskets of red-and-white flowers accented with evergreen had been added to the many poinsettias, while dozens of tall, flickering candles flanked the fireplace and the windows overlooking the mountains.

Once Camille and Matthew had decided they wanted to be married on Christmas Eve, Maureen and Vivian, along with Peggy, had all pitched in to help with the planning. Camille had made a whirlwind trip to Tucson and found the perfect dress of blush pink lace that brushed the floor and exposed most of her back. Instead of a veil, she'd adorned her upswept hair with a cluster of lily of the valley blossoms.

Vivian had stood as Camille's matron of honor, while Emily-Ann and Peggy had served as her bridesmaids. Blake had acted as Matthew's best man, with Holt and TooTall being his two groomsmen.

The men had all ribbed Matthew about finally being out of his chaps and jeans. Holt had even warned the crowd that the sight of Matthew without his spurs on might just cause the ceiling to fall in. Actually, Camille had never seen him in dress clothes, and when she'd gotten her first glimpse of him in a dark Western cut suit and bolo tie with a turquoise slide, his handsome image had very nearly taken her breath away. His untamed mane of blond curls glistened like gold in the candlelight, and as Camille had gazed into his gray eyes and repeated her vows of love, she could only think how far her life had come and what a blessed circle it had made to put her at Matthew's side.

So many friends and family had traveled from Three Rivers and Dragoon to watch Camille and Matthew exchange their wedding vows that the room was bulging at the seams. Now that the matching gold bands had been exchanged and Matthew had placed a meaningful kiss on his new wife's lips, the champagne was flowing and Christmas music drifted over the joyous crowd.

"For my beautiful daughter and new son-in-law," Maureen said as she thrust a pair of fluted glasses at the newly married couple.

"Thank you, Mom, but I can't drink the champagne," Camille told her.

Maureen looked at Matthew and winked. "Just like

I've forgotten that she's carrying your baby." She forced the drink in Camille's hand. "It's ginger ale, honey. So enjoy."

Camille leaned forward and kissed her mother's cheek. "Thank you for remembering, Mom."

She laughed. "How could I forget? You two have made me so happy. And by the way, Matthew, I have a bit more good news for you. Blake has finished the negotiations for the land. If all goes smoothly he'll be signing the papers next week. Ten thousand more acres to go with the thirty-five thousand you already have here. Even if it's across the northern boundary road, it will still be Red Bluff property. Unfortunately we couldn't talk the owners of the adjoining east property into selling, but who knows, if we keep offering them a good enough price they might come around."

"That is good news," Matthew told her. "So I guess this means more barns, more cattle and cowboys, and plenty more horses for Red Bluff."

Maureen affectionately patted his arm. "More everything. I'm going to miss the heck out of working with you every day, Matthew. But I'll get over it. Especially knowing how happy you've made my daughter."

Matthew slipped his arm around the back of Camille's waist and pulled her close to his side. "I'm going to do my best to keep her that way, Maureen. As for Red Bluff, it's going to be a pleasure to help it grow."

Before Maureen could say more, Vivian rushed up and took her mother by the arm. "Mom, I hate to do this to you, but Reeva needs you in the kitchen for something."

Maureen rolled her eyes. "I told Reeva we should've

had the wedding dinner catered, but she wouldn't hear of it. She just had to do the cooking herself."

Vivian shared a knowing glance with Camille and Matthew before she said to her mother, "She was insulted that you even mentioned such a thing, Mom. Camille is the last Hollister to get married and you think she'd let some other cook do the dinner? Only over her dead body."

Vivian tugged her mother away and Matthew used the moment to draw Camille to an empty corner of the room where the noise of the wedding crowd wasn't quite so loud.

"I know, I know," Camille teased. "We should have made the trip to the courthouse in Bisbee and let the judge marry us in his chambers. I admit it would've been a lot easier and quieter."

Bringing his mouth close to her ear, he said, "And miss seeing you looking so gorgeous and having all our friends and family here? Not for anything. You deserve this celebration, my beautiful wife."

She turned her head just enough to kiss his cheek. "Have you looked in at the dining room?" she asked. "The tables are decorated with flowers and candles and crystal, and Mom brought her best flatware and china down from Three Rivers."

He smiled at her glowing face. "I could eat Reeva's prime rib off a granite plate and be just as happy."

She laughed and then looked back out at the crowd. "Peggy and Gideon and Edie seemed to be enjoying themselves. I'm glad. I want them to feel like a part of the family."

"I believe they do," Matthew commented. "And Emily-Ann seems to be especially enjoying herself. I'm glad she could make it to the wedding. I know you two have been friends forever."

"Yes. And she caught my bouquet! You know what that means," she said, her eyes twinkling suggestively.

Matthew chuckled. "Now you sound like TooTall making predictions."

"Well, Emily-Ann deserves to have someone in her life. Like we have each other."

Sighing, she turned and was about to place a kiss on Matthew's lips when Holt suddenly strolled up with a short glass of bourbon and cola in his hand.

"Uh-uh. None of that, little sis," he teased. "You're an old married woman now. You can forget the hanky-panky."

She gave her handsome brother a tight hug. "What are you doing with that stuff?" she asked, pointing to the tumbler. "In case you didn't know, you're at a wedding. You're supposed to be drinking champagne!"

He laughed and winked at Matthew. "My system couldn't stand the shock. And speaking of a shocker, we just got one from Mom a few minutes ago. Did she mention anything to you two?"

"You mean about the land purchase to add to Red Bluff?" Matthew asked, assuming that was the only thing Holt could be talking about. "She told us the deal was going through and that Blake would sign the papers in a few days."

"Actually, it's been ages since I've seen Mom this happy," Camille told her brother. "Something has definitely lifted her spirits."

Matthew cast his wife a tender look. "I like to think she's happy about us and the baby. I realize that we surprised her, but she seems to be content with having me for a son-in-law."

"Oh, there's no doubt that she's over the moon about you two and the baby. But there's something else going on," Holt said. Then, moving closer, he lowered his voice. "She just told me and Joe that Uncle Gil has just retired from the Phoenix police force. And that's not the least of it. The man is moving to Yavapai County to live."

Wide-eyed, Camille glanced at Matthew, then back to her brother. "Is this for real, Holt? Or have you been downing too much of that bourbon?"

Frowning, Holt lifted his glass, "This is my first and last. And what I'm telling you is very real. Seems as though Uncle Gil called Mom this morning to wish her a Merry Christmas. That's when he gave her the news."

"Hmm. Wonder if this has anything to do with the investigation of your father's death?" Matthew pondered out loud. "After all, the man was a detective for the police force for years."

Holt shrugged. "All of us brothers are wondering the same thing. But Mom refuses to discuss the matter with us anymore. If Uncle Gil has solving Dad's death on his mind, then he's not going to get any help from Mom. On the other hand, she seems thrilled that he's going to be living close by."

"How close?" Camille asked, picking up on the suggestive tone in Holt's voice. "On Three Rivers?"

"I have no idea. But I guess we'll find out soon enough."

Beyond Holt's shoulder, not far from the Christmas tree, Camille caught sight of Isabelle standing with Gabby and Sam. Isabelle's baby bump was clearly evident beneath her bottle-green dress, and Camille could only hope she looked that lovely once her pregnancy grew to the advanced stage. Next to her, Gabby was close to Sam's side, and as Camille studied the old cowboy from afar, she realized she'd never seen him looking so dapper in pressed jeans, a white shirt and a dark vest. Cupid had obviously struck him with an arrow, Camille thought. And considering the man's much younger fiancée, he and Gabby were a testament that love wasn't always conventional. Which made Camille wonder even more about her mother and Gil.

"Excuse me, you two," Holt spoke up. "I'd better go find Isabelle. I promised to dance with her tonight."

Camille laughed. "Where are you going to find the space to dance in this crowd?"

Holt gave her a wicked grin. "We don't need much space. As long as I have my arms around her and we sway a bit, she'll consider it dancing."

As he walked away, Camille let out a good-natured groan and Matthew chuckled.

"Wow, it's still hard for me to picture Holt married and with a baby on the way," she said fondly, "but I'm so happy for him."

"And he's happy for us," Matthew thoughtfully replied. "Our sons or daughters will be cousins close to the same age. Who would have ever guessed that would happen?"

She gave her new husband a clever smile. "Uh— TooTall might have already guessed it. You think?"

With another chuckle, Matthew plucked the glass from her hand, and after depositing it on a nearby table, he pulled her into his arms. "I think Holt had a very good idea. We need to dance."

He maneuvered her backwards and through the door leading into the dining room. The space was blessedly empty of people and Matthew took the opportunity to place a lingering kiss on her lips.

"Merry Christmas, my beautiful wife," he whispered.

She smiled up at him. "Merry Christmas, my darling husband."

He gently moved her to the music and she rested her head against his shoulder. "Matthew, do you think Mom is romantically interested in Uncle Gil?"

He was silent for so long that she finally lifted her head to see a sheepish expression on his face.

"What?" she prodded. "Tell me."

"Okay, I can't really say how Maureen feels about Gil or any man. But Holt and Chandler seem to believe she's fallen in love with the guy."

Camille regarded him with mild surprise. "Hmm. Uncle Gil? I wouldn't have expected him to be on Mom's mind. Not in that way."

"Does the idea bother you?"

Shaking her head, she touched her fingers to his cheek. "A few months ago it might have. But now that I have you and our baby on the way, I understand what love really means and how it's made my life truly whole. If Mom can find that again with Uncle Gil, then I'll be the first to congratulate her."

He rubbed his cheek against hers. "I'm very proud of you, sweetheart."

Her heart overflowing with happiness, she held him tighter. "Our baby truly is a Christmas miracle, and tonight on our wedding night, nothing is going to dim the bright star shining down on Red Bluff." She brought her lips next to his ear. "You've given me the best gift ever, Matthew. Even if I have to wait a few months to unwrap it."

"I'm glad you think so. But how am I going to find you a gift for the following Christmases that will match up to this one?"

Easing her head back, she gave him a pointed look. "You don't think we're going to stop with just one, do you?"

Laughing, he whirled her in a full circle. "Camille, living with you is going to make every day seem like Christmas."

* * * * *

Be sure to look for Stella Bagwell's next book,
Fortune's Texas Surprise
the second book in the Fortunes of Texas:
Rambling Rose continuity,
available February 2020.

And for more Men of the West stories,
try these great books by
Stella Bagwell:

Home to Blue Stallion Ranch
His Texas Runaway
A Ranger For Christmas

Available now wherever
Harlequin Special Edition books
and ebooks are sold!

WE HOPE YOU ENJOYED THIS BOOK!

HARLEQUIN®

SPECIAL EDITION

Open your heart to more true-to-life stories of love and family.

Discover six new books available every month, wherever books are sold.

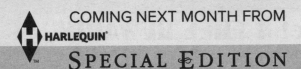

Get 4 FREE REWARDS!

We'll send you 2 FREE Books <u>plus</u> 2 FREE Mystery Gifts.

Harlequin® Special Edition books feature heroines finding the balance between their work life and personal life on the way to finding true love.

FREE Value Over $20

Love Harlequin romance?

DISCOVER.

Be the first to find out about promotions, news and exclusive content!

f Facebook.com/HarlequinBooks

🐦 Twitter.com/HarlequinBooks

📷 Instagram.com/HarlequinBooks

📌 Pinterest.com/HarlequinBooks

ReaderService.com

EXPLORE.

Sign up for the Harlequin e-newsletter and download a free book from any series at **TryHarlequin.com.**

CONNECT.

Join our Harlequin community to share your thoughts and connect with other romance readers!
Facebook.com/groups/HarlequinConnection

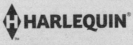

HARLEQUIN®

ROMANCE WHEN YOU NEED IT